DEATH AT DARK WATER

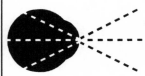

This Large Print Book carries the
Seal of Approval of N.A.V.H.

DEATH AT DARK WATER

JOHN D. NESBITT

THORNDIKE PRESS
A part of Gale, Cengage Learning

GALE
CENGAGE Learning™

Detroit • New York • San Francisco • New Haven, Conn • Waterville, Maine • London

GALE
CENGAGE Learning™

LIBRARY OF CONGRESS CATALOGING-IN-PUBLICATION DATA

Nesbitt, John D.
   Death at dark water / by John D. Nesbitt. — Large print ed.
     p. cm. — (Thorndike Press large print western)
   Originally published: New York: Leisure Books, 2008.
   ISBN-13: 978-1-4104-1343-7 (alk. paper)
   ISBN-10: 1-4104-1343-8 (alk. paper)
   1. Artists—Fiction. 2. Murder—Fiction. 3. Large type books.
 I. Title.
PS3564.E76D43 2009
813'.54—dc22   2008045456

Published in 2009 by arrangement with Leisure Books, a division of Dorchester Publishing Co., Inc.

Printed in the United States of America
1 2 3 4 5 6 7 13 12 11 10 09

For Roberto Garcia, compadre.

Chapter One

As the buggy approached the first adobe houses on the edge of town, Devon leaned forward and asked in Spanish, "Is this Tinaja?"

"*Sí,*" answered the driver.

Devon sat back in his seat. The ride from the train station had taken nearly a whole day, with very little to break the silence, and he felt as if he had lost track of time and space. If the driver had told him that Tinaja was yet a long ways off, he would not have known the difference. But now he was here.

He spoke to the driver, still in Spanish. "I have heard that this area has not changed much, that people still do things the way they did in years past."

"That's true."

"Good."

The driver shrugged. "Very little happens in this place."

"That is well enough, also. I hope to find

peace and quiet here."

The driver nodded but did not answer.

After several hours of seeing only flat desert plains and far-flung mountains, Devon appreciated details that were close enough to observe. A little girl no older than six stood with a length of jute twine around the neck of a tan goat. The animal, which had a beard hanging down and a pair of horns curving back, looked at him with bulging eyes as he passed. Next he saw a husky man, straw-hatted, leading two gray pack burros. The man had dark features and a bristly mustache, and he carried a switch about a yard long. After that, between two buildings in an empty lot strewn with broken blocks of adobe, two groups of boys stood facing each other. Just before they passed out of sight, Devon saw that the front boy in each group held his arm curled around a rooster. Fighting cocks. The one he saw better had long black tail feathers.

A water tank made of mortared stone came into view on the left, and as the buggy wheeled past it, Devon looked down into the dark water but saw nothing of shape or form.

The buggy came to a stop in front of a stuccoed building with a large wooden step. The driver climbed down, waited for his passenger to do the same, and then lifted the two traveling bags from the vehicle. Devon, feeling dazed now that the vehicle had come to a stop and he stood on the ground, stood and watched as the driver carried the bags up onto the wooden step and through the doorway. Devon glanced at the silent people to his right and left, then followed the man with his bags. Just before going through the double door, he looked up and read the sign: Los Ermitaños. The Hermits. It was the only sign he had seen so far in the town, and it served to remind him that everything would be in Spanish from here on out.

The driver set the bags on the dark tile floor in front of the reception desk, then stood back and lingered. Devon realized the man was waiting for a tip, so, remembering the long trip and the bit of work on each end, he fished out a quarter and thanked the driver. Then he turned his attention toward the tall, dark-featured man behind the counter.

"In what way may I help you?"

"I would like a room."

"Just one person?"

"Yes, I am by myself."

"Alone. For how many nights?"

"Several. At least a week."

The man paused. "Oh, you are here to visit?"

"Yes. I am an artist, drawing and painting. I like the solitude and the landscapes."

The man's eyebrows went up. "Oh, there is much of that here."

"That is very good." Devon motioned with his chin toward the counter. "Do you wish me to sign in?"

"No, this is a small inn. We will know you."

"And to pay?"

"When you are ready to leave."

Devon drew a five-dollar gold piece from his pocket and laid it on the counter. "Let me give you this as a surety."

The man barely looked at it.

"Do you serve meals?"

"Oh, yes. Do you care to eat now?"

"In a little while."

"Very well." The man showed a skeleton key and then hit a bell that gave a loud ping. "Federico will show you to your room."

A short, lean man in a dull white shirt appeared. He took the key, lifted the two bags, and walked toward a hallway that led deeper into the building.

Devon followed, turning when the man did and then taking one slow step at a time as the man banged his way up a stairway. Down another hall that ran parallel to the

10

one below, the man stopped at a door and clacked the key into the lock. He pushed the door open, carried the bags into the room, and set them on a foot rug. Then he stood back half a step.

"Thank you," said Devon as he gave the man a dime.

"At your service." The man handed him the key, then closed the door behind him as he left.

Devon crossed the room to the window, pushed the curtains aside, and looked. As the low mountains shimmered in the distance, he thought, this was what he had come for. Vastness, solitude, melancholy — as in the old poems about the country churchyard and the deserted village. Far from the madding crowd's ignoble strife, where an unseen rose might waste its fragrance on the desert air.

Two oil lamps had been lit when he entered the small dining room. He sat a table, alone in a quiet place — or almost alone, for as he looked around he saw a painting of the Virgin of Guadalupe with her radiant, shell-like background, and in an unlit corner of the room he saw a pale bird, something like a cockatiel, shifting on its perch in a wire cage.

The man who had carried his bags to the room appeared with a small, drab towel on his suspended forearm. "Do you care for dinner now?"

"Yes."

"Very well. I will bring it."

"Do I have choices?"

"The cook prepares the meal of the day."

From the gender of the noun, Devon imagined a woman with her hair in a single braid, stirring a large pot. "That's fine," he said.

A few minutes later, Federico returned with a large steaming bowl. As he set it down, Devon saw chunks of meat and boiled grains of hominy.

"¿Sopa?" Soup?

"Pozole."

The waiter left. He came back in a minute with a small plate of diced onions, shredded cabbage, and sliced radishes in one hand and a cloth bundle of corn tortillas in the other. He set the things down and stepped back. "Something else?"

Devon touched the plate of cut-up vegetables. "Does this go in the *pozole?*"

"Yes. Do you wish for anything else?"

"Is there beer?"

Federico gave a sad look. "No, there isn't. But if the gentleman wishes, there is a place that dedicates itself to that." He drew his brows together and nodded. "Not far away."

Devon smiled. "After the meal, then."

"Anything else for the moment?"

"No, thank you."

"*Provecho.*" Enjoy your meal.

Devon stood at the bar and drank a glass of beer. He supposed it was early yet, as only two other men were in the cantina. One of them, the bartender, was a large, round-shouldered man whose left eye twitched. He didn't say much and stayed at his end of the bar. The other man, not very neatly dressed, was strumming on an instrument very similar to a mandolin and getting settled on a stool against the wall. He had not shaved, or been shaven, for a few days, and his hair hung straight down in the style of a page boy in an old painting. From his movements and his appearance, Devon surmised that the man was blind.

The cantina was not without its decorations. On one wall hung a pair of heavy spurs with rowels bigger than silver dollars, and on another a rattlesnake skin, six feet long, had been spread out and tacked to a plank. Behind the bar, tied in a coil and hung from an ancient square nail, hung a braided bullwhip.

Within a little while, a man in a brown corduroy jacket and trousers sauntered into the cantina. He called out a greeting to the barkeeper and took a place a few feet away on Devon's right. After a smile and a nod to his neighbor, he spoke again to the man behind the bar, who set a bottle of tequila and a small glass on the bar top.

The man in the brown suit poured himself a shot of liquor and took a small sip. Then he turned to Devon and said, *"Buenas tardes."*

Devon, knowing that *tardes* stretched into the early evening hours for many people, returned the greeting.

"Are you visiting here?"

"Yes, I am."

"Oh, how good." The man smiled.

"It is very peaceful here."

"Oh, yes. Sometimes a wedding, or a baptism, and certain fiestas on saints' days, but very tranquil."

Devon noticed the man's large, expressive eyes and then his wavy hair and drooping mustache, brown but not very dark. He had a generally handsome look to him, in spite of a rough complexion. Devon took him to be younger than himself, between twenty-five and thirty.

The blind singer ran through a verse or

two and stopped, then took to plucking the strings and tuning his instrument some more.

Devon's new acquaintance called out, "*Ándale*, Juanito, don't sing only your songs of misery and sadness. Something lighter." Then he turned to Devon and said, "Do you stay at the inn here?"

"Yes, at Los Ermitaños. I imagine it's the only one in the town."

The other man gave a short laugh. "Oh, yes. There is only one inn, one cantina, and one church."

"Apparently they don't compete. I asked for beer at the inn, and they told me I had to come here. Even though it was night already and this place has no sign, I found it right away."

"It is not hard."

"I heard music."

The man laughed again. "Even if there is no music, and no laughter, I can find a place like this with my eyes closed."

"Especially if it is the only one in town. Does it not have a name?"

"It is called La Sombra."

Shade. Shadow. "For summer days?"

"Exactly." Another smile.

After a moment or two of silence, the man asked, "And do you come here just for the

15

weather, or are you looking for something?"

"I guess you could say I am looking for something."

"I do not know of any legends of lost treasure nearby here, although men have disappeared into the far mountains." He gave an appraising glance. "And you do not look like a miner."

Devon laughed. "No, I am not, although I like solitude and could imagine wandering the desert with a burro."

The man's eyes opened, and he smiled. "Oh, yes. Very pensive." After a pause he added, "But are you looking for something that is lost?"

"Perhaps better put, I am looking for something that is lacking, something I hope to find."

"Oh, yes? How interesting."

"You see, I like to draw and paint. I am looking for likely subjects to study."

"Excellent."

"I have heard there are many old buildings in this region, from the early days, off by themselves and alone."

"That is what you wish to find?"

"It is what I would like to study, to contemplate. From that I may discover something that seems to be missing. Within me."

"Ah, I understand."

Devon wondered if he did, but it didn't matter very much anyway. The conversation was a pleasant one. "So is it true that there are such places?"

"Oh, here and there, some of them far away."

"How far?"

"Oof!" The man waved his hand upward.

"And the closer ones?"

"Oh, well, there is an old church, fallen in and in ruins now, but in the kind of location you speak of."

"Really? And where is it?"

The man shrugged, as if he were hesitant. "Well, it is on the land of what used to be a large hacienda. Now it is called Rancho Agua Prieta."

Dark Water Ranch. "The ranch, that is, where the church is located?"

"Yes."

"And how might I get there, to ask permission? Do you know the owner?"

Again the shrug. "Well, yes. Actually, the people are relatives of mine. The main road east of town will take you to the ranch, and from there they can tell you how to find the church. If they are not bothered by your asking."

"Huh. Are they somewhat difficult?"

17

"Oh, no," came the quick answer. "But it is a large ranch. They have many things to do."

"Of course. And the name of the owner? How is he called?"

"The master of the rancho is Don Felipe Torres. He is the one who gives the orders there." After a short silence he asked, "Do you have a way to get to the ranch?"

"Yes, I do. Before I came over here, I spoke with the innkeeper, who referred me to the stableman, and I arranged to have a horse available."

"That is good. It would be too far to walk."

"And your name?"

"Carlos Hernández. *A sus órdenes.*" At your service.

"Devon Frost. *Mucho gusto en conocerte.*" A pleasure to meet you. With the formalities and the friendly handshake taken care of, Devon asked, "Shall I tell him I met you?"

Carlos made a small frown and shook his head. "He is married to my aunt for these several years, but he is a little bit special, and of late he does not receive me very well. So it would be better not to mention me to him. With my aunt and with my cousin, there would be no problem."

From the gender of the noun, Devon understood that the cousin was a female. "Very well," he said with a smile. "All serious with the *patrón.*"

"Just as well." Carlos took a sip of tequila and turned to the blind singer, who had yet to sing his first song. "*Ándale,* Juanito," he called, "Sing the song about the peach with the red heart."

Juanito strummed it out and sang in the voice of a man who confessed that he was bad but ate the peach all the same. He ate it all the way to the pit, or *hueso.* The stone of the peach was called a bone in Spanish, but the words of the song did not create an image of a red bone for Devon. Rather, he imagined he could look into the center of the peach and see its red stone heart. Juanito sang that song and many others.

CHAPTER TWO

Rancho Agua Prieta came into view first as a clump of treetops in the distance, then as a cluster of buildings in the midst of a vast plain. As Devon surveyed the country stretching out in all directions, he reflected that at one time the hacienda would have had all of that land and more in its dominion. And even if it had shrunk from a Spanish land grant, the ranch would still be big. Carlos had said *"muy grande,"* and the headquarters matched that idea.

Devon followed the road as it led to the main entrance, still half a mile distant. On each side of the gateway stood a stone wall, sloping down from six or seven feet high to about four. He could see now that leading away from each side of the entryway, an adobe wall enclosed the whole compound, high enough to keep out livestock but low enough for a couple of straw-hatted figures to peer over. To the left of the gate, a grove of cottonwoods showed their bushy tops, while to the right, a lower growth of pale green trees, perhaps acacia or locust, refracted the morning sunlight that came down from the far side.

At about twenty yards from the gate, Devon stopped his horse and dismounted. A dark man in drab clothes and a peaked straw hat came out from behind the stone wall and stood behind the two pole gates where they met in the center.

"¿Sí, señor?"

"I would like to speak with the *patrón,* if it is possible."

The man raised his head in a small gesture of challenge. "On the part of whom?"

"I am an outsider. He doesn't know me. But I would like to ask him permission for something."

"Just a minute." The man turned to his left, spoke to someone behind the stone wall, and then walked out of view toward the buildings.

A few minutes later, another man appeared at the gate, loosened the chain in the middle, and stepped into full view. He was a well-built man, above average in height and square-shouldered, with large brown eyes. Wearing a hat of palm fiber with a tighter weave than the first man's straw hat, he stood straight up with his head tipped back and his left thumb in the pocket of his brown leather vest. He had a toothpick sticking out of the corner of his mouth, and his smile showed a set of large teeth, one of them lined in silver. From the way he carried himself, as well as from his style of dress, Devon took him to be some kind of foreman.

"And how may I help you, sir?"

"As I mentioned to the other man, I would like to speak with the master of the rancho."

"The master is a very busy man. Might I ask what it is about?"

"Certainly. I am a visitor, as you can see. I am an artist, one who draws and paints. I have been told there is an old church on this ranch, and I would like to ask permission to study it and do pictures of it."

The man moved the toothpick around in the corner of his mouth as he looked over the stranger. "Do you not have a letter of introduction?"

"No, unfortunately I do not. But I assure you I am a man to be trusted." Devon held his hands away from his body, as a way of expressing that he went unarmed. "A simple artist."

The other man flicked his eyebrows.

"Come along."

Devon, leading the horse, followed the man into the headquarters of the rancho. Straight ahead, on the other side of a hard-packed bare area, stood a row of structures with one continuous roof. On the left end, an open wagon shed adjoined what looked like the main living quarters. To the right of that, a large set of double wooden doors suggested a *portal,* or covered entryway. After that came a storeroom of sorts, a carriage room with its doors open, and a corner area that, from the stovepipe sticking out of the wall, Devon took to be servants' quarters.

Along the right side of the compound, again under one long roof, lay a row of stables. At a glance, Devon took in horses that ranged in color — white, gray, tan, brown, black — about a dozen in all. He heard hooves thump against planks, and a couple of horses looked out to neigh at the newcomer. Up ahead on his left, a man in a black outfit stood holding a rope and pivoting to his left, while on the other end of the line, a white horse with a flowing tail trotted in a circle. The horse's steps made a light *tock-tock-tock* that stood out against the irregular sounds of the horses in their stalls and of someone, in a shop against the left wall of the enclosure, beating metal upon metal.

As Devon and his usher approached, the man in black drew the white horse in close and led it to a heavy snubbing post, where he tied it short. The foreman walked up and exchanged a few words with him, then stood aside as the *patrón* took measured strides toward his visitor.

"Buenos días," he said as he took off a pair of brown leather gloves.

Devon returned the greeting as he gathered his first impression of the master of the rancho. Although the man had been working in the sun and dust, he seemed dressed for a role he had set for himself. He wore a broad, ornate sombrero, deep black, to match his embroidered jacket and trousers and his polished boots. His pearl-gray shirt was in tone with the rest of his wardrobe, all of which was set off by a black gunbelt and holster, plus a riding quirt draped by its thong on the hammer of his pistol. He was a full-chested man, still in good shape in his mid-forties or so, with dark hair and mustache. He showed a set of full, even teeth when he spoke.

"Alfonso tells me you would like to see some parts of the ranch."

"Yes, sir."

The man had prominent cheekbones, and now his dark eyes hardened as he fixed them on Devon. "And what part calls for your attention?"

"An old church I have heard speak of. I am an artist, you see, and I am attracted to things of antiquity, the picturesque."

The *patrón* tipped back his head. He was taller than average, perhaps an inch or so taller than his foreman, and with his sombrero he looked even more so. He had apparently learned to use his height as a way of dominating other men. "So you like the old things?"

"Yes, sir. To observe them, to study them."

"Just to look, nothing more?"

"No, to draw them. That is how I study. One way, at least."

The eyes narrowed again. "Perhaps I should ask your name. How are you called?"

"Devon Frost."

"And where is your family from?"

"My parents, may they rest in peace, are no longer living. I have one sister, who lives in Ohio."

"O-hi-o," he said in three syllables. "And your own family? Children?"

"Not yet."

"You are alone."

"Yes, I am single."

"And you come on this trip by yourself?"

"That, too."

The *patrón* tipped his head to one side and then back. "I suppose so. Alfonso will show you where the church can be found."

"Thank you, sir. Yours is a generous gift to the arts."

"It is my pleasure." He gave a tight smile. "And your name again?"

"Frost. Devon Frost."

The man gave a blank nod, as if it still meant nothing, but he put out his hand. "Felipe Torres Real. At your service." Then with his spurs clinking he turned and walked back toward the white horse, pulling his gloves on as he went.

He spoke a few words to Alfonso as he walked past. The foreman nodded and started off across the bare earth toward a building adjacent to the blacksmith shop. Devon imagined it to be a bunkhouse, and his guess was confirmed when Alfonso came out buckling on a gunbelt. He crossed the ground within a yard of Devon without saying a word, then angled to the second-to-last stable on his right. There he took a rope halter from the wall, went into the stall, and came out leading a dark brown horse. He led the animal along the front of the stables and then, just past a stone water tank that stood out in the open, he headed across to what Devon had guessed to be a storeroom between the *portal* and the carriage shed. He tied the horse to a hitching rail, went into the room, and came out carrying a saddle and blanket.

Devon turned around so as not to be watching either the foreman or the *patrón.* He saw now that in the small grove of cottonwoods near the front wall, patches of sunlight glinted on a pool of water. In no hurry, he wandered over in that direction with his horse trailing along. When he reached the trees he could see that the edge of the pool had been lined with rocks in some earlier period of time. Now they were grown into the earth and were covered with dark moss where they touched the water. The pool itself, some twenty feet wide and thirty feet long, lay still and dark. He supposed it was an artesian pool and probably the basis for the name of the ranch. Agua Prieta. Dark Water.

He turned from the pool and looked again at the layout of the buildings, which seemed bright and glaring now. Someone had taken a lot of trouble, at one time, to haul in all the beams for uprights, cross members, and roof poles. The stable had been built in stages, first with milled uprights and crossbeams and then with round logs. All of the roofpoles in the compound were round, from six to ten inches thick, and with each segment that was built, it must have taken wagon loads of lumber to lay down a base for the dirt roof. Not much grass grew out of the top, which looked like packed white clay. That, too, must have taken innumerable man hours, not to mention draft animals and creaking carts. Devon doubted that the current master thought very much about how the buildings had been spliced and seamed together to give him the parade ground where he commanded his horses.

Alfonso had his mount saddled now. He walked it out a few steps, checked the girth, and swung aboard. With what felt like more effort, Devon pulled himself up onto his own saddle and then fell in behind the foreman.

The man who had first appeared at the gate now opened it, and the two horsemen passed through. Devon heard what he thought was the call of a peacock, but when he listened closer, all he heard was the metal clanging in the shop. Then he heard only the hoofbeats of the two horses. As the animals picked up a fast walk, dust rose from their tracks. Devon looked up and around at the open plains. Maybe Don Felipe thought his quest was trivial, but he hadn't come here to find out what others might think of him. The thought cheered him, and it saved him from having to think about anyone else in return.

Alfonso stayed long enough at the church ruins to roll a cigarette in a corn husk and light it. As he did so, Devon caught a glimpse of a peculiar feature on the man's saddle horn. The pommel, which was made of wood, rose up straight and round, and it seemed to have been etched and daubed into an effigy of a human head. Before Devon could get a better look, however, Alfonso kicked his horse into a lope and headed back in the direction of the rancho. Devon was left alone to ponder the roofless adobe walls of the old ruins.

It was a large church, he thought, for a location such as this. The high front wall, or façade, with its modest tower and windowed arch that once held a bell, would have risen above the original roof. There had been a narthex or anteroom, then a nave and a raised choir area. Along each side of the rear half of the building, lower walls showed where the roof had sloped down over small utility rooms. In back of the church but connected to the main building lay a set of three rooms, presumably the priest's chambers and a sacristy. The middle of these three rooms had a stone fireplace with dirt and debris collected in it.

All of the lumber except the door and window frames embedded in adobe had been taken away. The front entryway would have had large double doors, and the other entrances as well as many of the interior passages would likewise have had wooden doors. The outer walls had framed window openings, some of them large enough to have had shutters the size of doors. All of this woodwork, plus the pews and any cabinets or shelves, had been stripped. Perhaps some of the better doors had found new homes, but Devon suspected that much of the lumber had been re-fitted for chicken houses and sheep pens, while a great deal of it would also have gone up in the smoke from cookstoves. As for the roofbeams and slats, he imagined they had gone on to various uses as well.

Faded grandeur, he thought. At one time, it would have been a point of pride for the hacendado, or landowner, to have been the main patron of this church. With his sense of noblesse oblige, he would have kept it plastered, painted, and varnished; at over a mile from the hacienda buildings, it would have been accessible to the peasants who worked for him and to any indigenous people the priests had been able to convert. The humble people would have come through these doors for their weddings, baptisms, first communions, and funerals.

Now the doorways were closed off with piles of rock, the better to keep out wandering animals. Preferring not to dislodge anything, Devon crawled in through a window opening.

After a short walk around the inside, where he saw nothing significant that he hadn't already seen as he peeked in through the doors and windows, he stood at the back door of the priest's quarters and looked out upon the empty plain. It must have been an impressive experience, back when this was New Spain and no one had even heard of the United States and the American dollar, to come to a place like this to do God's work. Most of those men, no doubt, met the challenge with grace and courage, but he imagined that every once in a while, one of them had looked out a doorway such as this one and had failed to see anything meaningful.

Thinking that he would make his first series of studies from the outside, Devon walked back through the church to the window opening he had crawled through to get in. When he reached that place, he was surprised to see a four-wheeled buggy with a dark canopy sitting about ten yards away. The driver, who looked like he could be an uncle or father to the gatekeeper of the rancho, sat relaxed on his seat with the reins drooping in his hands. Behind him, but not fully in view, sat a woman.

Uncertain as to what kind of greeting to call out, Devon reached into his pocket for his penknife. Holding it sideways between thumb and forefinger, he rapped the end of it against the hard, dry wood of the window frame. The sound resonated, and the driver looked up. Devon waved. The driver turned and spoke to the woman beneath the canopy.

The driver got down from the carriage and waited to assist the woman. She leaned forward, but before Devon could catch a look at her face, she opened her parasol and held it out in front of her. Devon saw a black shoe, the long skirt of a blue dress, a ruffled sleeve, and then the upper body of a young, shapely woman.

What struck him at first was her light complexion in contrast with her dark hair, which was pulled straight back, wrapped in something like a bun, and held by a dark red clasp. A pair of hard, shiny earrings matched the color of the clasp, as did her lipstick.

"Buenos días," she said, taking a couple of steps toward him.

He returned the greeting through the window space.

"Are you the artist?" she asked, using the formal pronoun *usted,* just as Alfonso and Don Felipe had done.

"Yes, I am." He took off his hat.

"How nice. It is good to have an artist come to Rancho Agua Prieta." A small silver cross glinted where it lay against her chest, above her bosom.

"Is this your rancho, then?"

She stood within four feet of him now. "It is the rancho of my father."

"Oh, yes. I met him earlier. He gave me permission to come here."

Her face hardened, as if it had turned to stone. "That was not my father. He is my stepfather."

"Pardon me."

"My father, may he rest in peace, is Vicente Cantera. This is his rancho, as it was his father's, and the father of my grandfather before that."

"It is a grand place."

"My father loved it very much. A blessing

from God, which he never forgot."

"That is very good. And with whom do I have the pleasure of speaking at present?"

Her face softened. "My name is Petra Cantera Reynosa."

He nodded in a half-bow. "My name is Devon Frost. At your service."

She took another step forward and held out her gloved hand. Devon reached across the window ledge and pressed his hand against hers, with his thumb on the back of her fingers. Then she stepped back.

"If my father was alive, it would give him pleasure to know that an artist had come to render this church. He had hoped in his lifetime to restore it."

Devon glanced at the high wall, where the plaster had cracked and fallen off in large patches. "It would be a great deal of work."

She said nothing for a moment as she stood with the parasol on her shoulder. Then she said, "Is this your first day?"

"Yes, I'm staying in Tinaja, at the inn. I hope to come out here each day and gather impressions."

"Will you make drawings first?"

"Oh, yes. I will make many drawings. Then, if I progress that far, I will decide which views to paint."

"Oh, how interesting."

"Excuse me," he said. "Let me cross over." He boosted himself up onto the window ledge, swung his legs across, and landed on his feet on the ground outside.

"You seem doubtful about your work."

"Not so much. But at the beginning of a study, I do not like to take for granted what I hope to achieve."

She made a light arch with her plucked eyebrows. "Do you have much experience with your art?"

He shrugged. "Some years. But it is difficult to measure in time alone."

She seemed to reflect on that for a moment. "Is that why you came here, then — for more experience?"

"That, I suppose." He looked at her, wondering if the conversation was sincere enough for him to go further. The expression on her face told him it might be, so he went ahead. "I wanted more experience, but something bigger than that as well."

She tipped her head beneath the sunshade. "Something bigger?"

He glanced toward the carriage driver, who seemed to be paying no attention "Yes. In spite of several years of practice, my work seems to be missing the big thing. I think of it as my vision, and I came here with the idea that if I absorbed enough of all of this"

— he waved around with his right hand — "I will be fortified."

"So that is what you want, to find what is missing."

"Yes. I want to find what I think is missing in my life as well as in my work. A view of things. A center. When I find it, it will give me the power to do things in a more definite way." Then, feeling as if he had said too much, he added, "Not a very grand adventure, I suppose."

"It seems somewhat daring to me, to come here where people are different, almost like a foreign country, so isolated."

"It was what I wanted. Something — elemental. And I felt equipped, as I speak the language."

"You speak well."

"Thank you. I know it is not perfect, but I can take care of myself." After a short silence he said, "But we have spoken enough about me. Tell me about yourself, your family, what you do."

She looked down, knitted her brows, and raised her eyes to meet his. "There is not much to tell. I have no brothers and sisters, although two of them died as infants. We were just my father, my mother, and I. Then my father passed away when I was a little girl, and my mother was left alone with the rancho. It needed the hand of a man, she said, and so she married Don Felipe. He has been here for about ten years, and he is the master. He gives the orders. It is much different from the days of my father."

"I'm sorry."

"That is the way things are. My mother gave it all up to him, and there isn't much to do about it."

"And yourself — do you study? Practice music?"

"I go with my mother. To church, to visit. Sometimes I read, but I don't care for it very much."

"Do you go to the fiestas, to the dances?"

Her eyes fell as a twitch crossed her face. "Hardly at all. My stepfather says that all the young men from here are very low."

"Is that true?"

"There are families who do not think so, and as far as that goes, my father would have had more right to say it."

"By being your father."

"That," she said. Then with a droll look she added, "And by not being low himself."

Devon almost lost his breath. To vary the subject, he said, "Don Felipe seems to be a great aficionado of horses."

"Yes, it is one of his great passions," she commented, as if she were speaking of avarice or gluttony.

"And what does the rancho dedicate itself to? Mostly livestock?"

"Cattle and sheep. My father raised great numbers of both, and the men still tend to them. That is what my mother lives from."

"But Don Felipe is the owner?"

"He is the boss, and what is my mother's became his. But my father, in life, provided for the future of his wife and daughter."

Devon could see that she clung tight to some ideas, just as she did to the handle of her parasol, which she seemed about to wrench with both gloved hands.

"Tell me what you know about this church," he said.

"The person who really knew about it was my father. All I know is what I have heard." From there she went into a general narrative of how the grandfather of a grandfather oversaw the building of the church and gave to it generously. The best priests came from Spain. They were men of learning and drank fine wine with her father's grandfather. Then the hacienda was divided up, and the town of Tinaja grew. The common people became very numerous, and the diocese built the church in town. Now she and her mother went to mass there.

"And do you have other family?"

"There are some aunts and uncles left, and many cousins."

"I think I met one of your cousins in town. Carlos Hernández."

"Oh, yes. He is my cousin." She smoothed her parasol and pointed the tip at a piece of exposed adobe block. "Tell me. When you paint, do you represent all the defects?"

"In my style, yes. I am a realist. I came here looking for things no longer perfect."

"Sad things."

"Melancholy, let's say." He made a motion with his hand. "Something to activate feeling."

She smiled. "That is good, to know your purpose."

At that moment, a motion caught Devon's eye. On the other side of the buggy, a dark figure had ridden up on a white horse. Devon was sure it was Don Felipe, but the man had his head tilted and turned away, and the large brim of the sombrero closed off the features of his face. Then the head turned, and Don Felipe looked down on him with an imperious gaze.

Devon made an inquisitive gesture toward Petra, who gave a flick to her eyebrows as if she were trying to ignore a hanger-on at a dance.

"It is very good," she said, her voice a little

louder than before. "My mother is glad to know there is an artist here. We have so little culture these days. I am sure she would like to meet you."

"It would be a pleasure for me, whenever it would be convenient."

"Why not this afternoon, then? When you are done with your study here, we can expect you at the house. To take something."

"Oh, that would be fine."

She called to the driver in a loud voice, to tell him they would be leaving in a minute. Then she turned to Devon again. "Do you have with you something to eat?"

"Oh, yes. I brought a bit of food and water. Don't expect me until after meal-time."

She lingered. "And what do you like to take for refreshment? Tea? Coffee? A cool fruit drink?"

"Whatever you have. I'm sure I will enjoy it."

She pulled at her gloves, shifted her parasol, and gave Devon her hand. "Very well, we will see you later. At the house."

"Certainly. And thank you."

As she walked back to the buggy and let herself be handed up, Devon thought he understood why she took her time to leave. It would be a way of telling Don Felipe she

would take her own good time. As for the
master of the rancho, he was already gone.

CHAPTER THREE

Rancho Agua Prieta was a satisfying sight, as it came into view right where Devon expected to find it. In no hurry, he sat relaxed in the saddle as his horse plucked along. From time to time in the last mile as he looked over the country, he let his gaze rest on the rancho. With the trees on the west side casting shadows in mid-afternoon, it had a peaceful look to it, and he saw no motion or dust rising from within the walls.

When he was within a quarter mile of the gate, he heard drumming hoofbeats off to his right. A rider was coming in at a gallop, angling across to reach the gate ahead of him. Devon noted the dark horse, then the cream-colored hat and brown vest of Alfonso. The man rode light in the stirrups, leaning forward, and as he cut in front, Devon saw that he was slapping his right boot with a short length of knotted rope. Alfonso let out a whistle and a sharp yell, more for effect than necessity, as the gate-keeper was already swinging one half of the gate inward.

Devon gave his horse a nudge to pick up the pace. The ranch hand was holding the gate open, and besides, Devon wanted to get a closer look at the wooden effigy on the foreman's saddle horn. He had barely glimpsed it earlier, and now that Alfonso had thundered by, Devon's curiosity was piqued again. He rode the horse at a lope until he reached the entrance, then slowed down so as not to raise dust in the yard.

He nodded to the gatekeeper as he rode through. As he expected, very little was moving inside the enclosure. The cotton-woods around the dark pool whispered as a faint breeze stirred the leaves, and the sound of a closing door carried on the air. Alfonso walked from the tack room to the dark horse, which stood barebacked and shiny where the saddle had been. The foreman untied the horse from the hitching rail and led it to the stone trough.

Devon rode through the middle of the yard, which again struck him as a parade ground with its packed dirt and its regimented layout. Ahead on his left, a powder-gray horse stood snubbed to the training post with a nondescript riding saddle on it and a burlap bag of grain tied across the seat. The horse stood still but gave Devon the wide eye as he passed.

By the time he dismounted and got the horse tied near the tack room, Alfonso was no longer in sight. On second thought, Devon untied the horse, led it to the water trough, loosened the cinch, and let the horse drink. Then he tied it to the hitching rail again and walked to the double doors of the *portal.*

The entryway was easily large enough for a carriage to pass through, and the left door had a smaller walk-through door built into it. On the frame of the inset door he rapped with the butt end of his penknife.

After a long moment, the door opened inward and a woman appeared. She had a plain face, drawn and creased, with her hair tied back, and she wore a servant's apron.

"Yes, sir?"

"I believe they are expecting me."

The woman's brown eyes swept over him, taking in, he was sure, his light hair and skin and his blue eyes.

"You are the artist?"

"Yes, I am."

"Very well. Please come in."

She stood aside and let him pass into the *portal,* a roofed entryway with the entrance to the house on the left and an open view of the patio straight ahead. His eyes adjusted to the shade, which reached out a few yards into the patio. Sitting by herself at a round table well within the shade was Petra, the young woman he had met earlier.

She rose from her chair and said, "Please come and have a seat."

Devon took off his hat and walked across the paving stones of the *portal,* noting an open door a few yards to the right and a dark tack room beyond it. Then he let his eyes meet Petra's as he took her hand in greeting.

"Please sit down." She looked past him to the servant and with less warmth said, "Consuelo, tell my mother the artist is here."

"*Sí, señorita.*" The older woman turned and went into the house.

As Petra sat down, she said, "My mother is about to finish her dinner. She won't be long."

"I should have come a little later. I was in no hurry."

She gave a light frown and shook her head. "Don't worry. She waits for him to finish, that is all."

"Oh. And you yourself have eaten?"

"Before."

"Ah. Very well."

She touched the hard, bright earring on her right. "And how did you find the ruins of the old church? Interesting?"

"Yes. It is all very much so."

"A lovely sadness," she said, without a trace of humor or sorrow.

"It is different for me than for you. I am an outsider, come to observe the picturesque."

"And to find your vision."

He flinched at having it repeated where someone else might hear it. "That's just an idea."

She smiled. "What harm is there in an idea? After all, so many people have none at all."

"Oh, I suppose everyone has ideas of some kind. As one of our writers said, if a man's thoughts are of oxen, his dreams will be of oxen as well. Don't you think? Even if a person has, shall we say, not very elegant topics of thought, at least he has them."

"So that he may dream of oxen." She gave a dry laugh.

"There are worse things. At least they are honest dreams, based on honest work." He thought of an open spot. "I am sure your father believed in the value of all work. After all, someone has to kill the chickens, clean

46

the stables, render the lard."

"You are right. My father tended to all the affairs of the rancho, and he made sure all his people had their proper jobs."

"I am sure he did it well."

"And he did it without a *caporal.*"

"A *caporal?*"

"The second boss."

An image of Alfonso and his leather vest presented itself. "Oh. A person to take care of the cattle and sheep."

"Yes, and to look into everything and tell the servants how to do it, even unto gathering the eggs and grinding the corn for tortillas."

Devon was tempted to ask about the saddle horn, but he decided to go at it less directly. "To oversee such a large ranch must entail a great deal of movement. Did your father have horses for himself to ride?"

"Oh, yes. Very fine ones. But not for show."

"Of course."

"Do you paint horses?"

"Not very much. But I do have a small interest in saddles."

"For painting?"

"Perhaps for a detail in a larger picture." He paused to look at her dark eyes and light-complexioned face. Her features were not so soft as to make him feel he was taking advantage of her. "Do you still have your father's saddles?"

"Oh, yes. No one touches them." She raised her head in the manner of a person who had a prized possession to show. "Would you like to see them?"

"It would be an honor."

She rose from her chair. "Come this way." She led him to the tack room he had passed earlier. It's dark," she said. "Let me open the door." She went inside, and a moment later the room was lit by daylight coming in through the front door.

Devon stepped into the room and surveyed all the gear. There had to be upwards of twenty saddles, ranging from old, dusty antiques to others, nearer the door, that were slick from recent use.

"These were my father's," she said, moving to the back of the room and pointing out a pair of saddles on racks jutting out from the wall.

The first saddle was a tall, rigid-looking affair with a high cantle and swells that made the seat look narrow and deep, then stirrups with thick *tapaderos* that hung low. It had inlaid silver across the cantle and along the skirts, as well as silver *conchos* for the saddlestrings and on the taps.

The saddle next to it had a similar build

but less ornament. It had leather rosettes instead of silver *conchos,* and it had a plain, round wooden pommel rising straight up. This one was no doubt lighter than the first one, but Devon guessed it would still weigh a good sixty pounds.

"Just these two?"

"He had others, more common, but he gave them to his trusted workers before he passed away."

Devon paused, uncertain how to answer. Then he said, "I am not familiar with that kind of pommel."

She shrugged. "There are many kinds."

He swept his glance over the other saddles in the room. "And the rest?"

She pointed to a row of half a dozen, all of them clean and shiny and of a similar style with large, flat saddle horns that reminded Devon of small upside-down skillets. The leather had been dyed in rich colors — one saddle was black, another ox-blood, another mahogany, another the color of honey.

"These are his," Petra said, motioning with her head toward the house.

Devon nodded as he wandered toward the rank and file of working saddles. "And these? They are for the cowboys and the sheepherders?"

"Yes."

He noticed curled saddle leather, a frayed belly cinch, a latigo mended with twine. There was a mixture of styles, ranging from the high and narrow to the low and flat. Some saddle horns were covered and wrapped in leather, some were of bare brass sticking up from the swells, and some were of the now-familiar wooden type. He meandered past a row of these saddles and then walked around to get a front view as he came back. Finally he saw the one he had seen before, a large wooden knob with human features carved into it. The eye sockets and the recesses of the grinning mouth were painted black.

"All very interesting."

"Do you have an interest in drawing one of them?"

"Oh, not right now. I often think of things a little at a time. But I thank you for showing them to me."

"You're welcome."

"Shall I close the door, then?"

"Yes, please. I will wait for you outside." She moved toward the door to the *portal.*

When they were seated again at the table in the patio, she said, "It is good that people take an interest in the old things. It is so easy for others to forget."

"Yes, things change. Before I came here, I heard that this was a place where things had not changed much, yet I can see they have."

"Oh, yes. In the days of my grandfather and great-grandfather, everything was more elegant — the clothes, the coaches, the servants. But little by little, the money ran out. My grandfather, who never had to work in his lifetime, realized that his sons would have to. He decided that my father would run the ranch."

"Was he the eldest son?"

"No, but my grandfather saw that he was the best suited. Even as a small boy, my father played with the bones left over from the *menudo* and *pozole*. He pretended that they were his cattle and sheep and horses. And he was good with numbers, always counting the sacks of grain in the warehouse or the animals in a herd."

"A good decision, then, on your grandfather's part."

"Yes. My father was attentive to all details. He built up the herds and restored the finances, and my grandfather and grandmother lived in comfort until the end of their days."

"A very good son."

"Very good, even though it meant some sacrifice, that he waited until later in life to

51

marry and to have his own house."

"That is worthy."

"He was a man of great principle. And he made sure that his wife and daughter would be provided for. He did not know, of course, that it would become the plaything of another man, all that he left, but he fulfilled his duty."

"A man to be admired."

"Would you like to see a painting of him?"

Devon wondered about going into the house with so little ceremony. "Well, I suppose."

"It is a small one. I will bring it. You are an artist. You will appreciate it." She rose from her chair and crossed the patio to a door he had not noticed earlier.

She was back in a couple of minutes, carrying a framed miniature about five inches by eight. "Here," she said, placing it in his hands. "He had this painted in the year before he died."

Devon tipped the portrait to see it in better light. The artist had done a good job of capturing an expression of dignity. The late Vicente Cantera had a steady gaze and a firm chin. His graying hair, receding on top, was neatly trimmed and combed. His bushy gray mustache, which came out to a point on each side, reminded Devon of a photograph he had seen of Porfirio Díaz, the president of Mexico. Señor Cantera wore a high white collar, a black tie, and a dark gray jacket. The artist had mixed his colors well, just as he had done with the dark brown eyes and the royal blue background.

"A handsome man," said Devon as he handed back the portrait.

"The best."

"Do you want to put it away?"

"There is no hurry."

"The sunlight, though it is not direct, is not good for a fine piece of work like that."

She raised her eyebrows, as if in mild surprise. "Is that right? I hadn't thought of that." She stood up. "I'll be right back."

For the few minutes she was gone, Devon gazed out through the open gate at the far end of the patio. A small orchard of fruit trees grew beyond the wall; earlier he had noticed their bushy tops, and now through the opening he could see the branches and their shapes. It looked as if the trees were cherry, peach, and plum, all of which would have born their fruit and been picked for this season. Now they seemed restful as they cast their shade.

Petra came out of the house and rejoined her guest at the table. "Still my mother does not come."

"It's all right. I'm comfortable here."

"She won't be long."

Thinking back on an earlier part of the conversation, Devon appreciated what went unsaid: that Petra did not eat at the same table with her stepfather, and that the master might be taking his time when he knew his wife was waiting to meet a visitor. With nothing to say about any of that, Devon let his gaze drift around the roofed area between the house and the tack room. He noticed something he had seen earlier but had not registered consciously. It was a rectangular cage with a wood frame and a screen covering, suspended from the roof-beams of the *portal* by thick wires.

"What is that thing there?"

"It is for keeping cheese. When the door is open, the air circulates."

"Oh, yes. That's good for cheese. I didn't think it was a bird cage."

"No. My mother does have a bird cage, though, with a lovely white dove. Sometimes Consuelo sets it out here in the morning."

"It must be pretty."

"Yes it is. Do you paint birds?"

"No, not much. Again, perhaps as a smaller detail, off to one side."

"Perhaps you would like to see Cucu?"

"Oh, please don't bother. I assure you, I

am not getting restless."

At that moment, the main door to the house opened, and a woman stepped outside. Devon rose to his feet, hat still in hand, as she approached.

His first impression was that she was an attractive woman, with a trim and well-kept figure. She had shoulder-length dark hair, combed back and ridged up in front, with a dark, even hairline across the top of her forehead. Like her daughter, she had a pale complexion that, with an upper-class sensibility, she no doubt kept protected. She wore a white blouse, closed at the neck, set off by a black jacket and skirt of a lightweight, linen-like fabric. Like her daughter, she wore a small silver cross that lay against the upper part of her blouse. As she came closer, Devon noticed her soft brown eyes and a pleasant smile that showed small, white, even teeth.

"This is my mother," said Petra, also standing.

"Emilia Reynosa Huerta de Torres, at your service." The woman held out her hand.

Devon took it in a light touch. "Devon Frost. The pleasure is mine."

"Please have a seat," said the lady. She looked around in back of her, where the servant Consuelo was hovering. "A chair, please." The older woman brought a chair from the *portal* and helped her mistress take a place by the table.

"What a pleasure it is to have an artist at the rancho," said Emilia.

"It is a great privilege for me."

"The artist is enchanted by the old things," Petra offered.

Emilia looked at him. "How nice."

"Yes, one appreciates their antiquity. Also, they give one an idea of how things might have been in the days of the large haciendas."

"Ah, yes. Those times were different. More formal."

"And the hacienda itself, much bigger."

"Yes, and better. They had the best of everything."

"And the buildings themselves?"

"Some of the originals are gone, but many are the same. In that respect, the haciendas in the south were always larger and more ornate, with fountains and flowers and beautiful gardens."

"In the south?"

"Yes, for example, Guadalajara and Puebla and Cuernavaca. The climate is much more favorable there for lush gardens."

"Of course." Devon realized she was

thinking of one continuous Mexico, from the site of the current rancho to the old colonial towns where the Spaniards built, or commanded to be built, their churches and government buildings and elaborate residences. "I have seen paintings," he said. "There are some very impressive buildings. Nevertheless, there are many interesting things to be seen here."

"To observe and to paint."

"Yes."

"He likes the loneliness," said Petra.

"Really?"

"There is an atmosphere to appreciate."

"Ah, yes. And you come by yourself?"

"Yes, I do. I am staying at the inn, in town."

"That's good. And you are from the United States?" She spoke of it as if it were another country.

"From the state of Ohio."

"Is your family there?"

"A sister, nothing more. My parents passed away a while back."

"Do you not have a family yourself — no children?"

"Not yet."

She smiled in an expression of sympathy, and with a nod of the head she said, "Then you are alone."

"For now. I am used to it. It is convenient for my work." Devon reflected on her conversation. She showed the usual interest in family, but as she asked the same questions her husband had, Devon interpreted that Don Felipe must not have chosen to say much about his own impressions.

"You are young yet. At some future time you can form a household."

"Thank you. I hope it is so." He ran a quick calculation. From the looks of the portrait, which would have treated its subject well, the late Vicente would have been over sixty, which would have put him around fifty when Petra was born. By comparison, he himself was young, even though at thirty-five he felt the danger that life was going to pass him by.

"He is still looking," said Petra, "to find his art."

Emilia smiled, as if it didn't matter whether she understood the full import of what her daughter had said.

"Explain," said Petra. "She is interested."

Devon hesitated. "Well, there is an idea that a man should make his mark in life. There is a saying that he should plant a tree, have a son, and write a good book. It is not said in what order. For me, it seems that I must settle some questions about my work and then tend to the hearth. Of course, I am not a writer, so the equivalent of a book would be a realized work, perhaps a major painting on display in a public place. But I need to gather my forces to do that."

"And the tree?" asked Emilia, still with her kind smile.

"Oh, I have planted several. I have done various kinds of work." He looked at Petra, as if he were now confessing. "I have tried to be an artist, but I have had to earn my own living."

"Oh, that's good," said Emilia. "Better than being a *conchudo,* like my nephew Carlos. He has never worked."

"And probably never will," Petra added. "But we care for him very much."

"Of course," said her mother.

The door of the house opened, and Consuelo, who had been standing a few feet behind Emilia, moved aside as the master of the rancho, already wearing his wide hat, stepped forward and closed the door behind him. His spurs clinked as he walked across the paving stones and stood between his wife and his stepdaughter. He drew himself up to his full height, in an attitude of towering over those who were seated. Petra, without looking at him, shifted in her seat so that she had more of her back to him.

The movement did not seem to faze Don Felipe, who raised a cigarette to his lips and took a drag.

"You know the artist?" asked Emilia, looking up at him.

Devon now saw a trace of sadness, or perhaps apology, in her eyes. He was struck with the inequity between husband and wife, even though they would be about the same age, somewhere around forty-five, and she had given the man his present status.

The master smiled, but his eyes did not soften above the high cheekbones. "Yes. Earlier in the day. And how did you find the church? Agreeable?"

"Yes, very satisfactory. Thank you."

"You are welcome."

Emilia, looking up again with a submissive expression, said, "Perhaps the artist could do a portrait of you, Felipe."

Another smile, and a twitch of the dark mustache. "I do not think I would be a worthy subject for such an effort."

The two women looked at Devon, who said, "I do not have much skill at that sort of picture. I would be afraid I could not do justice to the gentleman."

Don Felipe smiled again, this time with more humor. "I would be too hard on your patience. Better for both of us this way."

Then, excusing himself, he went out through the *portal,* his spurs clinking and the quirt swaying from his pistol hammer as a cloud of smoke trailed over his shoulder.

"Is it true," said Emilia, now turning to Devon, "that you do not do portraits?"

"I have not found any talent for that."

"Not even for a picture of my mother?" asked Petra.

Devon smiled to Emilia, who now looked embarrassed. "Do not fear. I will not subject anyone to my inadequate treatment."

"You are too modest," she answered.

"You are too kind." As he said it, he saw the same trace he had seen earlier but could not identify — a mixture of apology and suffering, or an expression of inadequacy for not having done well enough and not being able to make amends. In that instant he admitted to himself that he would never be able to capture such an essence in a painting. Much better to stick to landscapes and still lifes.

Consuelo returned to stand a few feet in back of her mistress. "Do you wish to take something, señora?"

Emilia, recovering some of the grace she had shown before her husband appeared, showed her pretty white teeth as she smiled to her guest. "What would you like, sir?

Something cool? A water?"

By that, Devon knew she meant a flavored water, probably with fruit. "That would be fine."

"Very well, Consuelo. A water of peach."

When the shadows had lengthened and the pitcher was almost empty, Devon thanked his hostesses and said he must be leaving.

"It is very fine that you come and visit," said Emilia as she stood and took his hand. "You are always welcome at this house."

"Thank you." He turned to Petra. "And thank you."

"My mother is sincere when she says you are always welcome. We hope you come again soon."

"It will be my pleasure." Warmed by their grace and hospitality, Devon took leave and made his way to the *portal.* There, hanging near the door to the house, was a wicker cage with a white dove inside. Petra must have mentioned it to Consuelo at some moment. It was a nice touch.

He walked out into the enclosed area in front, where his horse stood at the hitching rail. Don Felipe must have finished his lesson with the gray horse and the sack of grain, for the rest of the yard was vacant.

Devon led his horse to the stone trough

for a drink, then tightened the cinch and mounted up. He pulled his hat brim down against the afternoon sun and put the horse into a walk. A light breeze riffled through the cottonwood leaves, and a few flecks of sunlight played on the pool of dark water. When he looked forward again, the gate-keeper had appeared and was opening the gate.

As Devon rode out onto the plains, he tried again to fathom the expression on Emilia's face. She had not always looked like that, he was sure — not when she was a young and pretty widow some ten years earlier, before the later changes came to Rancho Agua Prieta.

Chapter Four

The dining room had the same subdued atmosphere as the evening before. At the edge of the soft light of the two oil lamps, the Virgin of Guadalupe held her benign pose on the wall, and beyond the suffused glow, the pale, smallish parrot gave an occasional cluck and shifted its position. Devon did not hurry with his meal, which consisted of rice, beans, and boiled stringy beef with red chile. He told himself again that this was what he had come for — to take things in slowly, appreciate them, and let the effects settle in.

After a day in the sunlight and dry air and then a washbasin of warm water, his face felt clean and tight. He had drunk over a quart of water, and that effect, too, was taking its time to sink in. He wasn't thirsty, but as often happened when he went on a long horseback or carriage ride, he felt like satisfying himself with a beer. Even that was a deliberate idea.

It was an odd sensation, he thought, to feel as if he was being restored when he hadn't been through any major ordeals to exhaust him. He had known men who, after a rigorous course of study, or a prolonged business failure, or a disastrous love affair, had felt the need to go away and stare at a lake, hover on the edge of the company of women, or enlist in a war. From the time he had set out on this venture he knew he wasn't putting anything behind him or nursing any sorrows that he carried along. Yet he felt he was like those men, in that he needed to push himself out of his torpid state. Coming to this insular world was as good an idea as any other, and better than going to sit in sidewalk cafés in foreign cities, but he wondered if he was attuned. The church ruins were interesting but had not called up any spark; Petra was young and pretty, but on both occasions he felt as if he was talking to her through a thick plate of glass.

He tore off a third of a corn tortilla, curled it, and picked up a bite of meat and beans. Now that he thought of it, there had been a couple of things that had awakened some feeling. One was the solitude, the lovely sadness, as Petra had put it, of being alone in the vast openness where so many people and things had passed into eternity. The other was the thought, or speculation, of what Emilia might have been like just ten years earlier, when she was the age that he was now, and of what might have caused her to take on the haunted look of a latter-day Jocasta.

In the more congenial atmosphere of the cantina, Devon relaxed with a glass of beer in front of him. The objects hanging on the wall — the thick spurs, the rattlesnake skin, the coiled bullwhip — lent a familiar tone to the place. Lalo, the round-shouldered bartender, did not offer much conversation to Devon, but he was outgoing with the other patrons, clapping them on the shoulder and exchanging lively comments as he served their drinks. Devon could not catch the drift of their remarks, but he appreciated the good humor.

Juanito, the blind singer, looked very much as he did the evening before, with his drab clothes and straight hair looking one day farther along since the last bath and clean-up. The stubble on his chin, likewise, suggested that soap and the razor touched his skin about once a week. Devon noticed that his sleeves were dirty, as if he had been leaning on grimy surfaces, and his fingernails were as dirty as a blacksmith's.

He played a song that Devon recognized from the evening before, a mournful ballad with a waltz rhythm, the kind called a *corrido.* It praised the brave horses that men rode into battle, and the patrons at the bar sang along. Rifle balls, cannon shot, valiant horses, dying for the *patria* — Devon did not know if it went back to the battles in which Juárez regained control from Maximilian, or to the war with the U.S., or to some idealized war. The past era itself did not seem to matter as much as the glory that was carried on in the song. From pictures Devon had seen and from accounts he had read, most of the soldiers went on foot, and many of them wore partial uniforms and peasant clothing, but in the song they were mounted, with rifle and pistol and saber, riding great-hearted horses into the maw of battle.

Devon had not yet finished his first glass of beer when Carlos came in. He stopped to shake hands and exchange greetings with the other patrons and to get clapped on the shoulder by Lalo the bartender. Carlos said something with a jaunty toss of the head, and jolly laughter rippled through the little group. Then Carlos moved down the bar.

Devon noticed he was wearing the same

brown corduroy jacket and trousers as the evening before, and the white shirt did not look freshly laundered. The man was clean-shaven, however, and his expressive brown eyes were clear. His wavy hair was combed in place, and his drooping mustache, of a matching chestnut tone, was tidy and clean.

Before calling for a drink, Carlos shook Devon's hand and patted him on the fore-arm, at the same time telling him what a pleasure it was to see him again. Then he signaled to the bartender and accepted the shot glass and bottle. He positioned the glass and poured a shot, all in a measured style suggesting that there was a form to be followed. He set the bottle on the bar top, rotated it a quarter-turn, and pushed it back a couple of inches. He did not touch the shot glass until he was done with the bottle; then he hoisted the *copita* and took a sip.

"Did you go out today?" he asked.

"Yes, I did. I went to the rancho, and Don Felipe gave me permission to visit the church."

"Ah, how good. And did you find it to your liking?"

"Oh, yes. Interesting. And calm. All very quiet."

"It is very good that they treat you well."

"Yes. I also met your cousin, and her

68

mother, your aunt."

"Very gracious, my aunt."

"Indeed. And very courteous."

"And my cousin, did she look well?"

"Oh, yes."

"It has been a while since I have seen them."

"Perhaps they would enjoy the visit."

Carlos gave a sigh. "It would be nice, but things are not as they used to be at the rancho, in the time of Don Vicente."

"Yes, that can be seen. It has its own atmosphere now."

"Very serious."

"Your uncle seems quite dedicated to his horses."

"It is a great *afición* for him."

"I also met his *mayor-domo,* or *caporal,* as I heard him referred to. It was he who showed me how to find the church."

Carlos lifted the glass in his deliberate way and took another sip of tequila. "Oh, yes. Alfonso."

Devon appreciated the noncommittal tone in Carlos's comments about the step-uncle and the foreman. "I wonder if you can tell me," he began, "about a curious little thing I saw."

Carlos raised his eyebrows. "Maybe I can. What is it?"

"This foreman, Alfonso, uses a saddle that has something odd. The pommel, which seems to be of wood, has been sculpted or worked so that it looks like a human face — more like a skull."

"Oh, yes," answered Carlos, in the comfortable tone that anyone might use in talking about local customs. "It is an idea that some of these men have. Men who do not have a war to go to but would like to defeat their enemies."

"Really?"

"It is an idea from the Chinese. Some of them, according to legend, mounted the actual skull of an enemy on the head of the saddle, and then it became the custom to put on smaller models. Symbolic ones."

"Huh. Do you think this fellow Alfonso is dangerous, then?"

"Probably not. I think he's more of a show-off, a kind of braggart or bully."

"He's a good horseman."

"Oh, no doubt. If he were a common peon, they wouldn't let him get on a horse."

"They?"

Carlos seemed to hesitate at bringing out the word. "My uncle. He who is married to my aunt."

"Oh, yes. And as far as that goes, he seems like a bit of a show-off himself."

"That he is, for sure."

"He doesn't need to put a little skull on his saddle."

"No, he has all the authority he wants."

"And, of course, he uses a different kind of saddle."

"He has several, but yes, his favorite style has a different kind of pommel."

Devon glanced at the bullwhip on the wall as he phrased his question before saying it. "Do you think he could be a little — mean, or disagreeable?"

Carlos raised his eyebrows, turned down the corners of his mouth, and looked at his glass. "Oh, I think it might be so."

"I thought he gave that impression, but I didn't know how much he might have been putting on."

"He puts on an air, all right, but I think his cruelty is sincere."

"Are they afraid of him, then — your aunt and your cousin?"

"Oh, no. I don't think so. He is not that way with them."

"He is certainly the boss."

"Yes, indeed. But he doesn't practice his — how shall I say it — physical threats with them. In fact, my cousin ignores him, almost snubs him."

"I thought I noticed that." Devon reflected

for a couple of seconds and then added, "Is it something I should look out for?"

"For yourself? I don't know. If all you do is make pictures of the church, he will treat you as if you were a priest. But in other things, he is very jealous, and quick to anger."

"Jealous? Your aunt is a very charming lady, but I don't think she invites ill-advised attention."

Carlos gave him a fixed look. "That is true. But it is not for my aunt that he is so jealous."

"Really? Then —"

After a glance to each side, Carlos lowered his voice. "For my cousin."

The gender of the noun made it clear that the cousin was female, and Devon sensed that it would be very ungallant to mention her by name in a place like this. "Oh, like the jealous father who hates all the suitors?"

"Something like that, but not entirely like a father."

"Ah-hah." The scene on the patio presented itself more clearly now — Petra's insolence, Don Felipe's insouciance, Emilia's suppressed agony. Then came a fleeting image of the master's furtive visit to the church. "Not a good kind of jealousy, then."

"No. It is actually dangerous." Carlos took

a sip of tequila and then added, "In more than one way."

"It is certainly not beneficial to those in that house — but has he shown this jealousy to any young men, any suitors?"

Carlos's face had taken on a troubled look, and now his eyes watered. "Oh, it is terrible," he said.

"Has he done something?"

As Carlos looked around again and then began to speak in a low, earnest voice, he seemed on the verge of breaking down. "Señor, I have been very much in love with my beautiful cousin. I love her, I adore her, I would die for her. From the time that we were children, I always hoped that some day she would consent to be mine. It is all that I wish."

Devon drew back after such a gush. Then, recovering his sense of courtesy, he said, "And does she return your interest, or does she have eyes for someone else?"

"It would be tolerable if the only difficulty were that she did not return my love. That, I could stand. I could try to convince her, I could hope that with time she would see my case."

"Is it such, then, that she rejects you?"

Carlos winced. "That is a strong word. But she takes me lightly, yes. And that much

I could withstand. But this man — her stepfather — has made things a hundred times worse."

"He intervenes?"

The young man hesitated, took a deep breath, and went on in a quavering voice. "He told me, in pointed words, to stay away from her. To forget about her, to harbor no illusions."

"That's quite a bit for a man in his position."

"That is not all." Carlos made a visible effort to still the shaking in his voice. "He told me that if I valued my life, I must stay away from the girl, for anyone who presumed to love her, or to try to court her, was in risk of losing his life."

Devon raised his eyebrows. "And you think he is capable of following through with that threat?"

"Señor, I am sure of it. He is obsessed with her, and with the idea of making her his."

Devon felt a chill in his blood. "That's extreme. And the girl? What does she think?"

"I believe she hates him, but she acts as if he doesn't matter one way or the other. She pays him no mind. And then, she goes out of her way to make him jealous."

"How?"

"With another young man."

"Really? So she actually does have interest in someone else? I wouldn't have guessed it."

Carlos shook his head. "I don't think she really cares for him. I believe she lets on, so that Don Felipe will be kept in a state of turmoil."

"Whew! And the young man?"

"Completely in love, of course, and certain that he's going to win out."

"Has Don Felipe spoken to him, then, in the way he spoke to you?"

"Oh, yes. The story is well told in these last several days, so I will not be breaking a confidence in telling it to you."

Devon shrugged. "Let things be as they should."

Carlos's voice was steadier now. "Very well. The young man is named Ricardo Vega. He is the son of another landholder, Don Francisco Vega, an old friend of my uncle Vicente, my aunt Emilia, and so on, from many years past. A short while after Don Felipe made his threat to me, Ricardo derived the idea that he had some hopes with my cousin."

"Do you think she gave him those hopes?"

"It may well be."

"At any rate, he saw himself as her suitor."

"Exactly. And then one day, about a week ago, he and his father made a visit to Rancho Agua Prieta."

"Indeed? And how were they received?"

"As they are old friends, my aunt received them well. She was surprised at their suit, but she called my cousin into the living room and asked her what she thought. As the story goes, my cousin said that she didn't oppose the idea, as she could no longer live in peace beneath the roof of the house of her father."

"Suggesting something?"

"To Ricardo and Don Francisco, I think it suggested that she resented her stepfather for having taken over what once was her father's."

"I see. And how did this story get around?"

"When Ricardo and his father returned to their own rancho, Ricardo told the story to his brothers, and there were working men present, so in very little time the story was well circulated."

"I imagine. Returning to the story, what was Doña Emilia's response to the case?"

Carlos let out a heavy breath. "She said that Don Felipe would be the one to decide."

Devon felt his own heart sink. "Oh, that's too bad."

"Yes, it is. Regardless of anybody's motives, that was the worst way to deal with it." Carlos raised his glass for another sip. "Anyway, Don Felipe came in at about that time, and the case being put to him, he went into a fury. He declared absolutely not, that his daughter was worthy of much better, that these cowherds presumed a great deal, and that they should leave at once. Don Francisco became indignant, and he stated, with pride, that his family had had their land for generations before Felipe Torres came from who knows where, and that there was no such thing as a step down for the daughter of Doña Emilia if she chose to accept his son. Ricardo then declared that all his father had said was true and just, that the lovely Petra had already accepted him, and that he would not rest until she was his."

"And Don Felipe, all this time in his spurs and sombrero, standing in the living room?"

"I imagine so. He ordered them out of the house, then followed them through the *portal.* Once outside, he told them, in definite words, that if either of them so much as set foot on his land, the man would do so at the risk of his own life."

"The same threat of death, then?"

"Yes, the same."

"And that was the end?"

"Not quite. My cousin appeared at the door of the *portal* and said to Ricardo, 'This is not my father. He cannot order me. I have already given you my decision.' "

"And Ricardo?"

"He told her, in front of Don Felipe, that he would come for her."

Devon gave a low whistle. "And all of this happened a few days before I walked in? No wonder I felt some tension. And how about this young man Ricardo? Has he retreated at all?"

Carlos pursed his lips and shook his head. "He is of that type who believes he can have his way. Stubborn. Proud. A little conceited."

"Does she love him?"

"Pah! No more than she loves me. But her saying so is enough. He has proclaimed to his brothers and to the working men that she has accepted him and that he will keep his word."

"Do you think Don Felipe is capable of keeping his?"

Carlos gave him a full gaze. "I believe he is capable. Whether he would actually do it,

I don't know."

"At the very least, I wouldn't think it would make the girl like him any more. Do you think that he really thinks he can have her, or does he just not want anyone else to?"

"Señor, he is a very hard man. And up until now, he has gotten everything else he has wanted."

"But do you not think that your cousin, with my respect, is also a very hard person?"

Carlos smiled. "That's very good. If it weren't for the presence of her stepfather, I would not think it such a virtue in her."

At that moment, the door of the cantina opened, and Devon turned to see a familiar figure walk in. Devon registered the brown leather vest and woven-palm hat, then the large brown eyes and broad smile of the foreman of Rancho Agua Prieta.

Lalo came out from behind the bar, and the two of them exchanged a hearty handshake and clapping on the shoulder. Alfonso said something, and Lalo tossed back his full head of hair, shot with gray, and laughed. Then with his left eye squinting he said something in return that made Alfonso's silver tooth shine.

"El caporal," said Devon.

Carlos tossed a glance that way. "Oh, yes."

With the conversation now at a lull, Devon looked around and noticed that a few other men had come into the cantina as well. One of them, a man in grayish-white peasant clothes, seemed to be hovering a few feet away from Carlos's elbow. Devon took a drink of beer, and when he set the glass down he realized the man had moved in closer.

"¿Una pequeña cooperación?" said the man, holding up his right palm. A small cooperation?

Devon looked him over. He was of average height, slender, and dark-haired. He had a long head and a narrow face; his dull features and dusty complexion reminded Devon of a primitive stone figure.

"¿Una pequeña cooperación?" he asked again. As he spoke, he showed stubby teeth. The brown eyes with their yellow whites roved over Devon, and the bristles on his chin moved up and down.

Devon gave him a dime, thinking it was the best way to get rid of him.

"Thank you, sir. May God bless you." The man bowed his head, then tipped it to Carlos as he backed away.

"Who is that?"

"His name is Cayetano. He's just a *conchudo.*"

80

"*¿Conchudo?* What does that mean, exactly?"

"It means a person who always lets someone else pay or do the work."

"He wears the clothes of a working man."

"He talks about work, but he does very little. Mostly, he asks for money or drinks. He always has a lot of gossip, which he shares, and then he expects something in return."

"He didn't offer me anything."

"That's because you're new. Next time, you won't be able to get rid of him."

Devon looked around and did not see the man. "Did he leave?"

"He'll be back. There's no other place for him to go."

Devon shrugged it off and went back to his beer. Juanito was singing a song about a man who went down to the river where the girls washed their clothes in the sunlight. He sang it in two voices — one with the young man trying to get the girl to go away with him, and the other with the young girl protesting, "Oh, no, señor," at the beginning of each reason she could not go.

"Tell me, Carlos, do the women ever come to this place?"

"To this cantina?" Carlos frowned and

shook his head. "Women don't come in here."

"Just men?"

"That's it."

"Where are the women, then?"

"The young girls? They go out on a stroll on Sundays." He gave a closer look. "Or do you mean the other kind?"

Devon flicked his eyebrows. "Just curious. I didn't see any women, and in some places you do."

"Do you want to meet them?"

"Oh, I don't know. It might be interesting to see them. In other places, there is a part of town where you can pass by, on foot or in a carriage, and see where the women stand in doorways or sit on the steps. Perhaps this town is too small."

Carlos laughed. "It would have to be a town much smaller than this one. I know of a place, a *salón,* where the women do not stand in a doorway, but if you knock on the door and they know you, they will let you go in."

Devon tipped his head back and forth.

"Do you wish to see it?"

"It would be interesting, at the least, to know where it is."

"Of course. To know."

"Is it far?"

"Oh, no. A few blocks. Do you want to go now?"

"No hurry. Let's have another drink first."

Devon kept track of the turns they made along the unlit streets until they stopped in front of a building that had a solid door and no windows facing the street. Carlos led the way up onto the step and tapped on the door frame. Devon could hear voices inside, but no one came to the door. Carlos tapped again and the door opened, casting a slant of light into the darkness. Then the gap widened a couple of inches more as a woman's voice exclaimed, *"Ah, Carlos, ¿a qué vienes?"* What do you come here for?

"I have with me a friend, a fine gentleman, who would like to know where the lovely ladies hide."

"He is your friend? Bring him in."

Devon followed his guide into the lamplit room. The woman who opened and then closed the door stood off to one side, where her high bosom seemed in danger of pushing out of the top of her low-cut dress. She had reddish hair and a wide face with thick features, nothing that aroused Devon's interest. She introduced herself as Mari-Elena and then called out to the other girls, who Devon imagined had withdrawn at the knock on the door.

Two women younger than the hostess came into the room and sat down, one on each of two divans that faced one another across the room. Carlos, waiting, gestured to Devon with a sweep of the hand. "Have a seat wherever you wish," he said.

Of the two young women, one had caught Devon's eye when she first walked in. She had shoulder-length dark hair, hanging loose, and though her dress was not tight, he could tell she had a snug figure. He sat by her.

She had soft eyes and a bronze complexion, red lipstick and a hint of rouge.

"You are not from here," she said.

"No, I'm not. I am from farther north and east."

"What is your name?"

"Devon. And yours?"

"Ramona."

"So nice to meet you." He took her hand in greeting, and it felt warm.

"And you are on vacation?" she said as she took her hand back.

"I came to see a few things. Landscapes and vistas. I am an artist. I draw and paint."

"Oh, how nice."

"I like to see many things. Carlos told me that there were good things to see in this place, and he was right."

"Carlos knows well."

"I believe it."

"And do you come just to look? To know the place, to meet the people?"

"Here?" he asked, pointing to the cushion of the sofa.

"Yes, here."

"Oh, I came to be acquainted. And if what I see is very interesting, I might wish to see more."

She had one leg hooked over another, and with the free foot she tapped his leg. "And what do you think?"

"Everything looks fine."

"That's good."

He lowered his voice, although he could hear Carlos engaging the other girl in light chatter. "How is it done here?"

"Regular. Like anywhere."

"One pays in advance? How much?"

"You have American money? One dollar."

"And what do we do?"

"We go to the room."

"Yes, I understand. But once we are there?"

"The normal thing."

"Do you take your clothes off? May I take them off for you?"

She gave him a glance of appraisal. "Yes,

that would be all right."

Everything went well. He felt competent. He did not fumble, and her clothes were not tight and stubborn. Her loose hair and soft touch blended with the flowing movement. Just for a moment as he closed his eyes he had a memory of hard red surfaces and stone walls, and then he lost himself in the soft motion. He did not lose all sense of identity, though. The long dark hair that lay on the pillow and that he touched with his fingers belonged to a woman called Ramona.

CHAPTER FIVE

At the church ruins the next day, beneath a broad and sunny sky, Devon had plenty to think about. Though his memories of the time spent with Ramona were very pleasant, they kept giving way to the more serious considerations raised by his conversation with Carlos. On the simplest level, he had to wonder if he had anything to fear for himself, and beyond that, he felt he had to be on the lookout for anything he might find himself at the edge of. And he wasn't sure how much real danger there might be.

In the clear light of day, Don Felipe's threats of death seemed bombastic. Making the declaration out loud, to a family member and then to old friends of the family, would almost guarantee that the man could not follow through. If the threatened suitor turned up dead, everyone would know right away who had done the deed, and the perpetrator would have to answer for it.

Gone would be his status as master of the rancho, along with all of his outer emblems of the sombrero, pistol, spurs, and fine horses. Furthermore, if he did have designs on the stepdaughter, he would be ruining his own chances. If the man thought it through at all, he would have to know that making good on his threats would be self-defeating.

Yet Carlos seemed to think the danger was real. Carlos, who appeared so self-assured when it came to greeting his fellow carousers, meeting a stranger, pouring a drink, and knowing his way among the back streets and dark ladies, lost his repose when he spoke of Petra and her jealous stepfather. Part of it could be the helplessness and self-pity of the lovelorn, but Devon was convinced that Don Felipe's threats had shaken the young man, and Devon could easily picture the master striking a menacing pose as he gave his ultimatum.

Even if Carlos's view was tinged with fear, he had said a couple of things that Devon took as reliable — that Don Felipe was capable of carrying out a threat, whether he actually would or would not, and that he had always gotten what he wanted and therefore might think he could have Petra. Carlos seemed to have formed those impressions rationally.

Devon shook his head. He could understand how a man might harbor private fantasies about a young woman, but he felt that the man's thoughts must be distorted if he believed he could beat down the young suitors and force the girl to be his. Still, there was a good chance he really thought that way — maybe in the enclosed little world of Rancho Agua Prieta, itself a capsule in this remote, isolated region on the plains of New Mexico Territory where people carried on as if in an earlier time and place, Don Felipe believed he could make the laws.

Still, there was strong resistance within the young woman, even if the master killed off the young dogs. Maybe he believed that in spite of Petra's turning her back to him, he could create an order in which she yielded and her mother acquiesced. Maybe he thought, in a more sinister way than the young suitor Ricardo, that if his will was strong enough and he insisted with the authority that was his, he would prevail.

Devon sat on the window ledge of the outermost wall and sketched a doorway on the other side of the utility room. This doorway framed another that stood diagonally across the nave, and that doorway in turn framed a window that stood on the opposite outer wall and looked out upon the plain. Each of the doorways had heavy wooden beams, gray and weathered, embedded to serve as the lintel, and the window on the far side had an arch of adobe blocks across the top. The window was set in an unplastered adobe wall, while both of the doorways were surrounded by irregular patches of plaster. Where the plaster had cracked and broken off, a sub-layer of adobe-colored mortar showed, and in some places, especially on the upper right side of the second doorway, the mortar had fallen away and the adobe blocks showed through. It was an inspiring arrangement, just as found — the stages of deterioration allowed by passive neglect, in contrast with the evidence that someone at one time had taken great effort to create a durable and aesthetically pleasing structure. In addition to that effect, he had found an intriguing perspective that seemed to place the viewer, at once, on the outside looking in and on the inside looking out. He did not know if he had the skill to capture and interpret it all as he envisioned it, but the opportunity itself was something to revel in. Alone, with only the occasional brushing sound of his picketed horse grazing outside, he felt that he was apprehending a fair portion of what he had come for.

The shadows moved as the light on the walls changed. He had shifted a couple of times to keep the sun out of the corner of his eye. Now he pulled his hat brim down on the left side. The second doorway, with its various textures of aged lumber, adobe, mortar, and stained plaster, was a perfect monument of decay and loss. In another half hour the sunlight would make it look too flat, and he wanted to catch as much of it as he could in this sitting. When this moment had passed, the scene wouldn't be any good until he came at it fresh again tomorrow morning.

A rumbling, nickering sound from the horse made him look around. A quarter mile off, making its way in a light wake of dust, was the four-wheeled carriage he had seen the day before, being drawn by the same sturdy dark horse. His pulse gave a little jump. Beneath the shade of the canopy he saw the contrast of dark hair and light complexion.

So much for the present study. But if he had to be interrupted, this was one of the better ways. He shifted his legs around and landed with his feet on the ground outside the window opening.

As the buggy came closer, Devon recognized the driver from the day before — white-haired and leathery-toned, dressed in common garb and wearing a coarse straw hat. Again he parked the vehicle about ten yards away, and Devon sensed an ingrained discretion on the part of the servant. He left the carriage close enough that the lady would not have to walk far or be beyond a safe distance, but he kept far enough away that he would not seem to be listening in. When he had the lady handed down and on her way, he climbed back into his seat and assumed his patient, self-effacing pose.

Petra, meanwhile, walked in her assured manner, with her head up and her parasol protecting her light complexion. Her hair was pulled back again, and she wore large, round, red earrings so burnished that they looked as if they could deflect bullets. Her eyes tensed against the bright day, and her mouth held a tight smile.

"Good day," she said. The small silver cross caught the sunlight where it lay against the light gray fabric of her dress.

He returned the greeting.

"I thought I might find you here. I came by merely to say hello and to see if you are all right." She held out her gloved hand, which he touched and released.

"Just fine. I haven't been bitten by any snakes or scorpions."

She gave her close smile again. "The dangers of being an artist who ventures out of door. Like scientists who die from exotic poisons and virulent diseases."

"I think my greatest danger here would be falling asleep and getting a sunburn."

She cast her glance toward the ruins, as if the two of them had done enough of trying to be clever. "And how do things go? Do you advance in your work, in your pursuit?"

"So-so. I am trying to comprehend it slowly."

"That is good. This is no place to be in a hurry."

"True." He motioned with his head toward the carriage. "Do you go out on an excursion with some frequency?"

"Not really. Most of the time I have nowhere to go. But with a visitor, it gives me something to do if I come by to say hello."

"Very nice of you to do so."

She gave a light laugh. "I, also, run the risk of very few dangers."

He gestured again toward the buggy. "You are fortunate to have such a dependable man at your service. Even on a short drive —"

"Yes, he makes it possible for me to carry out my caprices." She glanced in the man's direction. "In truth, I have great trust in Miguel. He and Consuelo have been with the family since my father was young."

"I have the impression that your father was well liked by his people."

Her eyes met his as she nodded. "He treated them all very well. They never lacked the necessities, and if ever there was a baptism or first communion, he gave something. And for those who lived at the rancho itself, he always had a piñata at New Year for the children. Miguel and Consuelo's sons and daughters are the age of my mother, and they still speak well of him when they visit."

"It is a great blessing to have had such a good father, or a father who was such a good example of a civic man."

Her eyebrows went up a little, and she tipped her head to one side. "He was not without his imperfections."

"I'm sure."

"In order to salvage the rancho, he had to take measures that some would criticize."

"Like a man of business."

"Somewhat. I told you that my grandfather did not work."

"Yes."

"He had been raised with the idea that he didn't have to. His was a life of leisure. Well, for many years, things had been breaking down little by little, because of this careless treatment. Some pieces of land were reclaimed by the families of earlier owners and then neglected. Other pieces were poorly managed and had great debts against them. My father was very persevering in his reunification of the ranch."

"By acquiring parcels."

She nodded and seemed to be staring at a point on the wall beyond him. "Yes. Some of it he did with payment, and some of it he did with legal process."

"By filing claims?"

"That, and lawsuits, and settlements."

Devon shrugged. "I trust that he was justified."

"Oh, yes. But he had good lawyers and he was a friend of the judge, so there will always be those who hold a grudge, who will say he took advantage of the system."

"But he preserved the rancho."

"Oh, yes. First, to recover what had slipped away in his father's time and before that, so that he could maintain my grandfather and grandmother in the comfort they were accustomed to. And second, to provide for the future of my mother and myself."

Devon saw little to be gained by sharing his impression that the sainted father may not have been entirely selfless in his objectives and methods. "That is an admirable achievement," he said.

"Yes, but there were things he was unable to accomplish. This church, for example." She motioned with her free hand toward the desolate walls. "It was his dream to restore it."

"It would have taken a great deal. Only the basic shell is here. Many things were stripped away over time, and much of the surface would have to be refinished as well."

"If God had granted him a few more years, he might have seen some success."

Devon nodded but did not change his idea of what a huge project it would be.

"But it was not God's will. Not to see this project realized, nor to see his family enjoy the later years in his own house, nor to see his daughter marry." She dabbed at her eye with her gloved hand.

Devon had a fleeting vision of Don Felipe giving Petra away in marriage, and the idea was so incongruous that it kept him from thinking of any other way of advancing the conversation.

"But enough of that," she said, widening her eyes and sniffing. "There's no remedy for what's in the past. My father loved his rancho very much, and the good thing is that it is still together."

"Oh, yes."

She tilted her head beneath her parasol. "And you, who come from so far away, what do you think of a place like Rancho Agua Prieta? Does it seem strange to you?"

"Not really. It has its own way of being. In English we have a saying that still water runs deep."

She sighed. "There are many truths in life."

He thought he should say something more. "It is interesting to know about the place, its history and all, to know how its fortunes have risen and fallen."

"Oh, yes. There is much history. But there is also some change that is disagreeable."

"Just from looking, a person would have little idea of anything in specific, other than change itself." He made a backward motion with his hand toward the church.

Her face took on a bit of a sultry look. "Perhaps so. But at the rancho itself, would a person not observe something?"

"It is difficult to say. If I had known nothing of the past, I can't say how much I would have observed about a change. From the outside, everything seems to be in its own order." He tried to give a goodnatured smile. "It is not, as they say, as if swineherds were living in the palace."

"It's not so far off. The contrast between this man and my father is so great, that I have noticed it and felt it every day for these past ten years."

"Yes," he said, still smiling. "But to one who had never known your father, the difference would not be evident, not on sight."

"Perhaps so. But wouldn't a person notice that ours is a house in which manners have some value?"

"Indeed. Courtesy and grace are immediately apparent."

"And this presumptuous person, this upstart?"

"Well, when I met him on the grounds outside the house, I would not have known a contrast. Because of his . . . pride. As I said, from the outside. But within the patio, yes, I did notice a difference in sensibilities. But you had already given me your opinion of him, also."

She laughed. "*Some* of my opinion."

He felt a small relief as he laughed in return. "And, of course, I did not go into the house."

"Oof!" she said, wrinkling her nose. "There it would be most apparent, with his habits that my father would abhor."

"Such as?"

"Wearing his hat and spurs and pistol in the house, and smoking at the table." She turned her head and gestured with it toward the plain, in the direction from which she had come. "Not to mention that."

Devon followed her glance and saw a lone rider poking along, a man in a light hat and brown vest, idling on a dark brown horse. "The *caporal*."

She pursed her hard red lips and flicked her eyebrows. "The same."

"The master sends him?"

She turned to put the foreman at her back again, and as she did so she raised her forefinger to tap her cheekbone below her eye. "He tries to manage always to have someone keep an eye on me." Then she twirled her parasol. "How foolish."

Devon looked beyond her for a second and caught a glimpse of the carriage driver, Miguel, drowsing on his seat. It made sense. Don Felipe could not depend on the older, loyal servants to report on the stepdaughter, and he was so urgent to keep her from having contact with Ricardo that he had to keep her under surveillance.

Devon sighed. The day before, he thought the mastermight be spying on her because of her visit to the artist. There may have been some element of jealousy there, as in the later scene on the patio, but as Carlos had said, as long as Devon was just making pictures, the master would treat him like a priest. A eunuch, in other words. Just an insignificant dilettante.

He brought his eyes back to Petra, who seemed to be waiting for him to say something. "It is the story of centuries," he said. "The jealous elder."

She raised her head in an expression somewhere between confidence and superiority. "To no purpose." She turned her gaze again at the church, this time to the upper walls. "I have taken up much of your time," she said. "You have your work. Time passes you by."

"To the contrary. No time could be better spent than in such amiable conversation."

"You are kind. But I must be going anyway."

Devon glanced out toward the plain, where Alfonso still loitered.

"Not for that," she said with nonchalance. "If it were only that, I would stay hours."

He laughed. "Well, it has been an enjoyable visit. I hope to see you again soon."

"A pleasure to stop by and say hello." She held out her hand. "Until next time."

As the carriage wheeled away, he was left to wonder whether she had come to see him out of interest or for the less generous motive of bedeviling Don Felipe and his foreman. That could account for her leaving so abruptly — to make Alfonso turn around and go back, and to give him nothing to report. Of course, there was the possibility that she had something to do at home. She wasn't the type to roll out fresh flour tortillas every day at noon, but maybe she needed to shake out a couple of white linen handkerchiefs for Consuelo to press.

In spite of her petulance, though, he was sure she was deeper than she let on. He found it interesting to consider what she had left unsaid. She had made a general comment, on her previous visit, that Don Felipe disapproved of the young men in these parts, but she gave not the slightest indication that she and her stepfather were embroiled in an argument, complete with death threats, over a suitor. Also, as she spoke of Don Felipe's habits in the house, she mentioned only his accoutrements and his smoking, not his tendency to crowd into a person's space or to stand over in a dominating posture, much less any other gestures, such as looking and touching, that the girl's father would truly abhor. She referred to only the most superficial aspects, yet she never implied that her contempt was limited to them. And the way she had turned her back on Alfonso, as she had done to her stepfather the day before, was something to appreciate.

Devon went back to his sketch pad and, seeing that the moment had passed for working on the perspective of the doorways and windows, decided to work on an entirely different view. He went out in front of the church to ponder the high wall with its empty belfry arch. He could not help thinking what a focus of attention it would have been for Petra's father, the late Vicente Cantera. Even if the man had never gotten past the stage of nurturing a pet idea, he would have looked at this wall and tower and would have thought what a fine image it would make with new plaster and paint and a stately bell.

It was hard to know, on the basis of Petra's praise, how strong Don Vicente's ambition to restore the church had been. But if he had rebuilt the rancho, and if had instilled a sense of pride and social class in his family, plus a yearning for the grace of an earlier era, all of which he seemed to have done, he might well have seen the church as an opportunity for a crowning achievement.

Devon could appreciate the ambition to restore a measure of quality. In the earlier days of the hacienda, in the colonial period, the residents would have seen themselves as a kind of New World aristocracy. Like the Europeans they read about, they would have had caged songbirds and artificial fountains. The women would have found seclusion behind the thick walls, to keep away from the common rabble, the dust, the wind, and the darkening sun. They would have read of women in Spain who had large bath areas in cool palace rooms, where they could lounge in deshabille while blind musicians played Arabic music, and they would have taken the trouble to have comfortable bathing areas while the summer heat raged outside. They would have had dances and receptions; they would have dressed for dinner. They would have gone out in closed carriages, and in good weather the ladies might have ridden their palfreys, groomed and caparisoned by the invisible servants. All of this and more the original *hacendados* would have practiced, emulating the best of their forebears, and members of later generations, like Don Vicente and Doña Emilia, who would like to recapture some of it.

Don Vicente fell short, however. Not being born to wealth but to the attitudes of those who had had it, he had so much to recover that he was unable to rebuild the church. Devon thought it must have loomed as too big a project, for there was not a visible point in which anyone had done anything. Perhaps Don Vicente had seen it as an all-or-nothing project and had not been able to summon up the resources and the energy to assay it. Nevertheless, he had done his part to preserve quality and class at Rancho Agua Prieta, and that was no small achievement in itself.

His successor, the current master of the rancho, apparently had his own sense of prestige. With land ownership, plus a household and graceful wife at his command, he could affect a kind of elite, equestrian-class status at the same time that he asserted his physical prowess as a tamer of horses and a performer of feats in the *charreada*. But even if he acted superior to his neighbors, and even if he could ride like Genghis Khan and wrap a steer's tail around his saddle horn, in the end he was a man who wore his sombrero and spurs and pistol in the house and smoked at the table. Petra had made that much clear, and Devon had a glimmering of what she did not mention: Don Felipe's ideas of manhood resembled those of a primal era if he thought that by taking over a dead man's estate and wife he had a right to take over the daughter as well.

Devon let out a long breath as he looked over the façade of the church again. None of this was his, and none of it was any of his business, but he was glad of one thing. Even if he never had a nickel to his name or never found a vision for his work, at least he would not give people like Petra a reason to call him presumptuous. He laughed. No, not even if he met a rich widow some day. He would have a sense of what was his and not his.

Devon sat in the dark cantina, savoring his glass of beer and keeping an eye out for Carlos. On the previous two nights, Petra's cousin had come in by now, but this evening he had not made an appearance. Three other men stood at the end of the bar nearest the door, and Lalo the bartender stood opposite them. Juanito had come in and was running through a few melodies but had not yet begun to sing any songs.

Devon looked around at the now-familiar decor on the walls and took another sip of beer. A voice at his right elbow caused him to turn. There stood the narrow-faced man he had seen the night before, the one called

Cayetano.

"Buenas noches, jefe," said the man. Good evening, boss.

"Buenas noches."

"Could you give me a little something, to help out?"

"I don't have any change." Devon observed the man's dull features and dusty complexion, and he wondered what thoughts went on behind the stone-like exterior.

"There is no hurry." After a pause the man added, "You are new in town. I can be your friend. If you need to know something, I can tell you."

Devon tried to think of something contrary, something to make the man not want to talk to him, but the best he could come up with was, "Where do you work?"

"I work wherever they want me. In the fields, with the livestock, making blocks of adobe." He tapped his chest. "I am very good for working."

"And right now?"

"The *maestro* I work for had to go to Artesia, so right now there is no work for me."

"I thought there was a lot of work right now."

"For the people who have work, but they are jealous. They don't want to give me a chance. Maybe the boss will fire them and keep me, so they tell the boss lies. And anyway, I have work, when the *maestro* comes back."

"I see."

"And you are the artist, aren't you?"

"Yes."

"I have heard of you. They say you are received at Rancho Agua Prieta."

"I have been there. They gave me permission to study the old church and make pictures of it."

"The rancho has much history."

"So I understand."

Cayetano was silent for a moment as his gaze fell on Devon's beer glass. Then he said, "I could tell you something."

"That's all right. I don't need to know anything more right now."

The man's closed mouth moved up and down, as if he was preparing to produce something. Then he said, "You like the pretty girl?"

"Which one?"

"The one at the rancho."

"She is very nice."

"You do not like her very much?" Now the man twisted his mouth to one side and opened his eyes wide, showing the yellow whites.

"I have barely met her. I don't have a reason to like her more than would be customary. She is very gracious." As an afterthought he added, "Like her mother."

"Oh, yes. They are a good family." The man shifted on his feet and moved half a step closer. "You are not in love with her?"

Devon tried to show his irritation with a frown. "No, not at all."

"That is good, because it is said that she is engaged to another."

"That doesn't interest me very much."

"A young man whose family has a big rancho. His name is Ricardo Vega. He can take her away."

Devon shook his head. "That's his affair, if he can. And hers."

Cayetano's face took on a leering expression now. "Perhaps you have heard that he said he would go for her. He told his workers. Everyone knows it, everyone is waiting for it."

Devon shrugged.

"This, in spite of what Don Felipe said, that if he set foot on Rancho Agua Prieta he would risk his life. Still, he says he will take her away, *at night*."

"Very well."

"At night, mind you."

"It's all the same to me." Devon tried to

ignore the man by looking around at the other patrons. Alfonso had come in, as had a couple of other men, but Carlos had not.

"Are you looking for someone?"

"It doesn't matter."

"Your friend Carlos?"

"I don't see him."

Cayetano came another half-step closer. "He may not come tonight."

"That's his choice."

"They have all been to the rooster fight. He lost his money there, and his mother gives him only so much."

Devon stared at his glass, still trying to ignore the man.

"You could ask Alfonso. He was there, and he won most of the money betting on the rooster called El Moro. That's why he is happy."

Devon fished into his pocket and brought out a dime, hoping it would get rid of the man. "Here," he said. "I found this."

"Thank you very much, sir. I know Carlos is your friend, and I am sorry Alfonso made him angry."

Devon waved his hand. "I didn't know he did. But it's just money anyway. Next week another rooster will win."

"Oh, it was not for the money that Carlos became angry."

"How, then?" As soon as Devon asked the question, he knew he had played in.

Cayetano smiled as he moved his long head from one side to another. "After he took his money, Alfonso made fun of him. He asked what kind of a man he was, to let Ricardo push himself in and be the *pretendiente*. Poor Carlos. Maybe it was the tequila, and maybe it was just Alfonso laughing at him, but he threw the bottle down on a rock and broke it. Then he shouted that Ricardo was a *fanfarrón*, that the girl didn't care a pea for him, and that he, Carlos, could assure them that Ricardo would not have a grain of success."

"And you were there?"

"Oh, yes. Everyone was."

"And Carlos?"

"He went away by himself. He will probably not show his face for a day or two."

Devon drank the last of his beer and pushed away from the bar. "It's too bad," he said.

"Are you going now, so soon?"

"I don't feel like having any more right now."

"Very well. Have a good evening, and thank you for your generosity."

"You're welcome."

"At your service, sir."

110

CHAPTER SIX

Devon sat on a cement bench that looked inward upon the town square. The church bells at the other end of the plaza had just tolled two o'clock, and the townsfolk were beginning to stir. Mass was long over, and the people had had a chance to eat and take a siesta. As Federico the waiter had explained it, Sunday afternoon was the time of *paseo,* when everyone went out for a stroll. Some went to visit family members, while others walked around the park. It was the day to relax, and the only people who worked were those who, like Federico, had to.

When Devon had come out to sit for a while, during the second mass, he had seen only one person on the street, a dark, thin woman dressed all in black and twisted with age, walking from the center of town to some street several blocks south, where she disappeared. Now people were showing up.

A short, round woman with a hand cart was setting up to sell flowers. A man with two burros laden with clay water jugs was unfolding a table. A couple of gray-haired, wrinkled men sat in silence on benches facing one another, and a heavy, middle-aged man sat on a low stone wall and smoked a cigarette.

The first girls had arrived and stood in a group of half a dozen at the far end of the park, and a young man in a white shirt and red bandana turned his horse down the street in their direction, passing on Devon's right.

A few minutes later, a young couple with a toddling little boy and a baby in the father's arms walked by. The boy ran ahead with his arms open, and two pigeons started up from the pathway.

Now came Juanito, with his hair clean and his face shaven. With his right hand he carried his instrument upright by the neck, and with his left he snapped his fingers every couple of steps. He was wearing clean clothes, and a straw hat hung at his back from a string around his neck. After he took a seat on a bench about ten yards from Devon, he pulled the hat free and set it on the ground in front of his feet. Then he began to pluck the strings and tune the mandolin.

A man with a short-brimmed straw hat and a clipped mustache came along with a pair of crossed sticks in each hand. A wooden marionette monkey dangled on each side of him. Smiling, the man turned to Devon and had the monkeys do a jig; then he went on his way, pausing every ten or twelve steps to let the monkeys bob and clatter.

Past the lady with the flowers and the man with the liquid refreshments, a woman with brown hair and a light complexion set out a small table and stacked it with creamy tan bars of candy, the kind called *jamoncillo*.

A couple of young men rode along together, again in white shirts and red bandanas. One of them had jingle-bobs on his bridle chains as well as on his spurs. The other had a pair of rich brown leather gloves tucked into the back waistband of his trousers. Both of them had gleaming, clean faces and the soft, dark beginnings of mustaches.

A vendor walked by with a mound of peanuts on a tray suspended by straps that crossed between his shoulder blades. Two boys aged eleven or twelve stopped him long enough to wheedle a handful of peanuts, and then they sat on the curb.

Another knot of girls had formed at the far end — young girls, from the looks of them, anywhere from thirteen to eighteen, all of them with full-length dresses and long, dark hair.

A wizened old man with a cane turned a milky eye toward Devon and then shuffled by. He sat at the other end of the bench from a man who had dozed off.

Now a couple of women appeared, older women who looked as if they might cook or clean. They wore shawls and ample dresses, and they took heavy steps in flat-soled shoes. They stopped at the table where the woman sold *jamoncillos.*

Juanito strummed the mandolin sharp and loud as he began to sing a song. It was a sprightly air about the swallows in springtime, building their nests in the eaves of the barn. Like young-hearted lovers with no thoughts of danger, each year they returned and went through it again. For the old men with sticks and the young boys with stones could not change the nature of birds wild and free. So come, my little pretty one, so dark-winged and lovely, oh come, my little pretty one, and fly, fly with me. Oh, come, my little pretty one, and fly, fly with me.

A few more couples with small children had shown up, appearing as if out of nowhere. The man with the marionette monkeys now had an audience of half a dozen children who let out little squeals and laughs. Voices floated on the air, as did the call of the man with the peanuts. In the background of these sounds came the slow clop of horse hooves when a rider passed. The park was beginning to hum, with Juanito's music a sharper and clearer element in the blend of sounds.

Suspended in the warm afternoon, as Devon relaxed his gaze and did not focus on any particular object, the park swam in a slow, flowing motion, like a theater audience as viewed from the wings before the curtain went up.

The smell of cooked meat wafted on the air, causing Devon to turn in his seat. A man and a woman stood behind a cart that had wisps of smoke rising from a grill. A large side of ribs — lamb or mutton from the looks of them — lay raw-side-up on the grate.

A group of three girls, walking abreast with their arms joined, came into view on his right. They were young and pleasant-looking, and they kept their gaze straight ahead. A few minutes later, they came into view again as they walked back the other way. Not long after that, another group came by. They did not turn around and go back but rather disappeared behind him and came into view again on his left as they continued all the way around the plaza. With the appearance of another pair of girls on his right, again coming from the other end of the park, he realized the promenade was under way.

In groups of two or three the girls strolled along, sometimes coming down one side of the plaza and sometimes down the other, sometimes turning around and going back and sometimes walking all the way around. Always, however, they stayed on the pathway along the edge, not far from the street. The young men rode up and down the street in similar patterns and variations, while their rivals on foot loitered here and there, leaning against a tree or perched on the back of a park bench. All of the young women were clean and neat, dressed for the *paseo,* and they all let on as if they were unaware it was going on. The girls chattered and laughed in their little groups, with only furtive, flickering glances to the side. The young men acted likewise, as if they had come by obligation to exercise their horses or to lend their presence to the shade.

Meanwhile the man with the peanuts and the woman with the *jamoncillos* called out their wares, the man with the marionettes made the children giggle, pigeons fluttered, Juanito sang songs of love and treachery, and the smell of roasting lamb fat carried on the air. From appearances, no one took notice of the *paseo* — not the woman with the flowers, not the couples with little children, not the old and slow and heavy people who wove in and out of the path of the señoritas on promenade. Later, Devon supposed, when the shadows lengthened and dusk drew in, some of the young women would break off from their groups and some of the young men would come within speaking distance, but in the height of the afternoon it was all a free-flowing *paseo* for everybody.

He awoke and blinked his eyes, trying to clear his head after having dozed off. The sun had not moved and the sounds had not changed, but he sensed something different. It was the tone of some of the voices.

A man holding a burro with a rope halter stood in the street and spoke in an energetic voice to the man roasting the ribs. Two other men, clean in their casual Sunday clothes, stood at the edge of the street and listened. Devon thought he heard the words for night, pasture, and dead, but he could not be sure. When the conversation came to a rest, there was a slow shaking of heads and a muttering of *"Ay. Dios mío. ¡Qué cosa!"* Oh. My God. What a thing.

For the next little while the news rippled from one party to another, two or three people at a time. Meanwhile the promenade went on, with the young men and women passing in random patterns and keeping a lookout for glances. Devon still could not catch the drift of the gossip, so finally he went to the liquid refreshment stand and ordered a glass of lemonade.

"Excuse me," he said as he paid the man. "It seems as if something has happened."

The man, who was about Devon's age and had the look of a responsible townsman, said, "Oh, yes. Something very grievous has occurred."

Devon nodded as an invitation to go on.

"You are the artist who visits Rancho Agua Prieta, aren't you?"

"Yes, I am."

"Perhaps you know the young lady of the rancho, then."

Devon narrowed his gaze as he felt his upper body tighten. "Yes, I know her."

"Well, she has recently attracted the attention of another landholder's son, one Ricardo Vega. Perhaps you have heard."

"Only a little."

"It is said that he went to the rancho to ask for her hand, but Don Felipe turned him away with a threat against his life. You may have heard that also."

"Again, just a little, nothing more."

"The story is told that he planned to take her away at night, in spite of the stepfather's threats. Last night he left his own house, not telling anyone precisely where he was going. But it was supposed that he went to Rancho Agua Prieta."

Devon tipped his head in half a nod.

"At dawn this morning he had still not come home, but his horse did, with blood on the saddle, so they went to look for him. They found him dead on the pastureland out on his father's ranch."

Devon felt a stronger tenseness in his midsection. "Dead?"

"Yes. With bullet holes."

"That is indeed very grievous."

The man shook his head in a slow motion. "It is a terrible thing for his family."

"I'm sure."

"A young man, strong and brave and full of life."

Though he had never met the young man, Devon could picture him — dark-haired in a clean hat and jacket, headstrong and impetuous. "It is a pity," he said. "A very sad loss."

"His family wants a complete investigation."

"With reason." Devon tried to pick his next words with care. "But are there different thoughts about who might have done it?"

The man raised his eyebrows and looked around, as if he did not want to be heard saying something indiscreet. "Of course, the person who issued the threat has to be considered, though it is hard to believe he would actually do it. He would expose himself to immediate punishment, and after all, he did not have much of a reason."

Perhaps in the public view, Devon thought. But he said, "Who could have a stronger one?"

The man widened his eyes again. "A jealous man. His rival."

"The cousin of the young woman?"

"The same."

Devon frowned. "He is not very probable."

"Maybe not. But he was heard declaring, not long before, that Ricardo would not live to make Petra his."

"Oh. I thought he said Ricardo would not be able to take her away."

"I was not there."

"Neither was I."

"But his boast, however he put it in words, leaves him under suspicion, at least as much as the stepfather's threat does to himself."

"That's unfortunate."

"Oh, yes. But the young man's family has a right to demand a full inquiry. And he has many brothers as well as his father. They will not let it go unanswered."

"Nor should they." Devon took a sip of the lemonade, which was tepid and sweet. In order to leave the glass, he drank the rest of it down. "Thank you for the drink," he said. "And for the information."

"You're welcome. May things go well for you."

Devon went back to his bench and sat down to absorb the import of what he had heard. He could not believe that Carlos had committed the crime; it just did not seem to fit. On the other hand, he was stunned that Don Felipe could have followed through with it, if indeed he had. Meanwhile Ricardo's family had the grief of losing a young man who had just begun to grab life by the horns, and as they mourned their loss, the rest of life went on in commerce, conversation, song, and wordless promenade.

■ ■ ■ ■

Devon tried the door of the cantina and found it closed. Dusk was falling and the park was almost empty of people, so he went to sit again on a bench. Left to his own thoughts, he pondered the sensation of sitting here alone and in quiet, in this place where a few hours earlier there had been a bustle of life and the rippling news of death.

A dusty-looking human form appeared on his left, and at first he did not recognize the person, partly because he did not expect to see him in this setting. But the details came together quickly enough — the slender build, the dark hair, the long narrow head like a dolichocephalic stone figure.

"Buenas tardes, jefe."

"Buenas tardes, Cayetano."

"Did you just come out?"

"No, I was out earlier, during the *paseo*. I came out again a little while ago, but it looks as if La Sombra is closed."

"Oh, yes. For being Sunday."

"So I thought."

Cayetano stood in a slouch, shifted his weight from one foot to another, then broke the silence. "Maybe you have heard the news, then."

122

"I have heard some."

"Of the death of Ricardo Vega?"

"Yes, I heard that. It is too bad."

"Oh, yes," said Cayetano, with a solemn up-and-down motion of his head. "It is a very bad thing."

"And it is not yet known who did it?"

"Still nothing. Of course, there are two who are the most suspected."

"So I understand. Do you think, really, that Carlos could have done such a thing?"

Cayetano put his hands together in a pious, supplicant gesture and moved his head back and forth. "Oh, I am no one to judge something like that."

The answer struck Devon as a mealy-mouthed way of saying that Cayetano would not mind believing, or having it believed, that Carlos might have done it. But Devon just said, "Huh. And others, what do they think?"

"I cannot say, not for others. But if Carlos had not said what he did at the rooster fight, there would be less suspicion on him at the present."

"And the other, the master of the rancho?"

Cayetano looked down. "Oh, it is a very serious thing to accuse a man of that class."

The obsequiousness irritated Devon.

"Does his wealth, or his status, put him beyond suspicion? Or are people afraid of him?"

"Oh, no, it's not that. But he is very proud. He would not go to someone else's rancho, in the night, to do that. He would do it in open day, in a challenge."

"What if the young man came in the night and died there? They could have carried the body back."

Cayetano shrugged. "It is not for me to say."

"What about the *caporal?*"

"Alfonso was in plain view at the rooster fight and then for the rest of the night in La Sombra."

"Who knows if there is a third party, then. But I cannot imagine Carlos committing such an enormous act. Where is he, by the way?"

"He is closed up in his mother's house. He does not go out today. They say he is afraid to show his face."

"That's too bad." Devon thought for a second. "Where does he live?"

"Do you want to see him?"

The man's eagerness was distasteful. "I don't know," said Devon.

"I'll show you."

"You can just tell me. This is an easy town

to get around in."

"I'll show you." Cayetano took a couple of sideways steps and motioned with his hand. "Come on."

Devon figured the man was angling for a tip, and it was either this way or some similar way to get rid of the nuisance, so he got up.

"It's not very far." The man shook his head in an expression of assurance.

Devon walked along beside his guide and made note of the corners and cross streets until they came to a wide adobe house set back from the street some thirty feet and facing north. The front patio was enclosed by a six-foot adobe wall with a wrought-iron gate in the middle.

Cayetano picked up a pebble from the street and used it to rap on the iron railing. After a moment of silence he rapped again.

The house door opened, and a middle-aged lady in a jacket and skirt appeared. "What do you want?" she called out.

"Good afternoon, with my best wishes, Doña Flora. Comes here a gentleman who would like to visit with your son Carlos."

The lady raised her head. "For what reason? Who is it who wants him?"

"The American artist. A man to be trusted."

"Just a minute. Let me see." The lady turned and went into the house. A minute later she reappeared. "My son says he will see the American. Tell him to come through the back entrance."

"Thank you, señora."

Cayetano led the way to the corner and back around through the alleyway, which was lined with weeds and piles of rubble. The two men came to an adobe wall on the left, and there at an iron gateway stood Carlos.

Devon fished out a dime for his guide, who tarried just long enough to wish a good evening and to assure Devon he was at his service.

Carlos opened the gate, and as Devon stepped in and shook hands, he saw that Carlos was not faring well. The man was dressed in a clean brown cotton suit, about the same tone as the corduroy he had worn earlier, and he had on a clean white shirt. He was well groomed and clean-shaven. But his face, with its rough complexion and large, expressive brown eyes, had a haunted look to it.

"Come and sit in the patio," he said, "where we won't bother my mother."

Devon followed him to a roofed area on the east side of the house, where the shadows lay heavy and the daylight was fading. Two chairs of wrought iron painted white sat next to a matching round table, and on the table sat a bottle and a glass.

"I'll bring a lamp," said Carlos. "And a glass, if you'd like one."

"Sure. Go ahead."

Within a few minutes, Carlos carried out the motions of a good host, and the two men sat, each with a glass of tequila in front of him.

"Very good of you to come by."

"I didn't really plan to, but Cayetano seemed to think he should show me, so I came."

"Very well. I'm sure he likes to feel useful, though he doesn't have much success squeezing money out of me." Carlos gave a small cough, and as he reached for his drink, Devon saw that his hand was trembling.

"Are you not feeling well?"

"It has been a difficult day."

"Yes, I was sorry to hear of the misfortune."

Carlos looked up, and his eyes were brimming with moisture in the lamplight. "In spite of everything, I am sure my cousin Petra knows I would never have done any harm to Ricardo."

"I guess that's one of the reasons I came to visit you, to tell you that I, too, was convinced that you could not have done such a thing."

"Thank you."

Devon shrugged. "It is difficult for me to understand how anyone, in seriousness, could hold you in suspicion."

Carlos, his eyes still moist, shook his head. "Yet they will. And it is all my fault."

"How so?"

"For the foolish thing I said at the rooster fight, when I was provoked by Alfonso."

"That was just talk, and the drink. I wasn't there, but I know that much."

"Yes, but I'm sure it has been exaggerated and distorted."

"All the same, if you came home after that and were here for the rest of the night, what can they say?"

Carlos heaved a sigh, and with a sad cast to his face he shook his head. "But there's the detail. I did go out."

"Really? I didn't see you."

"Not to the cantina. I went to Rancho Agua Prieta."

It was Devon's turn to exhale. "Is that right? For what purpose?"

Carlos shook his head again. "It sounds so stupid. But the moon was bright, as you will see it again in a few minutes, and I had a yearning to see the rancho. I did not hope to see my beautiful cousin, only to see the rancho and the light at the window, to know that she was there inside and to be that close to her."

"So you went?"

"Yes."

"Not on foot?"

"Oh, no. I took a horse from the stable where we keep them."

"So a stableman saw you come and go?"

"Yes, though it would be nothing to lie about any way. I rode out there, saw nothing except the ranch itself, and no one saw me. I achieved what I set out to do, which was to see the house beneath the moon with my beautiful Petra inside, and I came back."

"How long were you gone?"

"Between two and three hours."

"And you were back, let us say, by midnight?"

"I would say so."

"Well, it may not look good, but like you say, it is nothing to lie about. And if you did, and someone found out, it would look much, much worse."

Carlos had tears starting from his eyes. "But that is how stupid I am, my friend. I have already told them I was at home, and then when they said they knew different, I had to admit it."

"Who is *they?*"

"Ricardo's brothers. Two of them came in the afternoon."

Devon shook his head. "Well, you just have to stick to the truth. This will all go to the law, won't it?"

"Oh, yes. I'm sure the sheriff will come to see me tomorrow."

"You just have to tell the truth."

Carlos's face clouded even more than before. "I am sure it is just a matter of time before they take me to jail, and after that, it is in the hands of God."

"Don't give up so soon."

"That's easy for you to say. The truth is, I should have given up much sooner."

Devon frowned. "Why? So what if you went to see her house in the moonlight? People in love are always . . . they always do things like this."

Carlos took a good gulp of tequila and shook his head again. "Sooner, much sooner. I should never have hoped."

"One must always hope. The only thing I can see is that she is your cousin. But everything else —"

"Oh, for that matter, being a cousin doesn't have much to do with it. It would

be difficult, here, to find someone acceptable who wasn't related in some way."

"Then why should you not have hoped?"

"Because the disillusionment is so strong."
Carlos lifted the bottle and tipped it toward
his guest.

Devon held out his hand, flat, and moved
it back and forth. "No, thanks."

Carlos poured himself a couple of ounces.
"Here it is. My brother went through the
same thing. He was in love with a girl — a
more distant cousin, actually — and he
wanted to be her *pretendiente.* But her
father said, no, not yet, the girl was too
young. Then came another *galán,* with his
parents, and they asked for permission for
him to visit. The father conceded, and the
young man had exclusive visiting privileges
for a year, which of course he took advantage of, visiting every Sunday."

"And during that time, no one else could
see her?"

"Not at all. And after a year, he came with
his parents again, and they asked for her
hand, and that was it. Within another year,
she was gone, living with him and his
parents, washing clothes with her mother-
in-law."

"And your brother?"

Carlos gave a most mournful look. "May

he rest in peace. He died of a broken heart."

As Devon understood it, dying of a broken heart often meant a relentless siege of drinking. "I'm sorry," he said.

"That's the way things are. From his example I should have learned. But when I heard that Ricardo had declared himself and swore he would carry her away, and my cousin old enough to go, in spite of the pain it would cause her mother —"

"You reacted."

"Yes, like a great fool. I made stupid remarks about Ricardo, and then I went to be close to her presence in the night."

"You didn't go to try to intercept him?"

"Oh, no. I wanted to see no one and for no one to see me. I hoped with all my heart he would not come that night, and I was glad he didn't."

"At least while you were there."

"Well, yes. Beyond that, I know nothing, except that things look bad for me."

Devon followed the streets in the moonlight, from the back gate of Carlos's house to the front door of the dark house where he had gone a couple of nights earlier. He was sure of the way and did not need a guide.

He rapped on the door frame with his knuckles, and the woman with the reddish hair and wide face opened the door.

"Yes?" she said.

"Good evening. I came here the other night, and my friend Carlos introduced me."

"Oh, yes."

"And I was wondering if your place is . . . open."

"It is Sunday. But if a girl would like to receive a guest, such as someone she knows, that is acceptable. Let me see."

She backed away and closed the door, leaving Devon to stand by himself on the doorstep with no light other than that of the rising moon. After a couple of minutes, the door opened and the woman appeared again.

"It's all right. Come in."

As she moved aside, Devon stepped into the lamplit room, where Ramona sat on a divan. His eyes met hers for an instant, until he was distracted by the sound of the madam clicking the latch on the door and then the sight of her disappearing through a set of curtains that hung in a doorway. He brought his gaze around to meet Ramona's again.

"Good evening," she said. "Would you like to sit down?"

"Thank you." He took a seat.

"And how goes your stay here in Tinaja?"

"Very well, I believe. I enjoyed sitting in the park this afternoon while everyone was doing the *paseo*."

"Oh, yes. It is very nice."

"Do you ever go?"

"Oh, no," she said. "I do not know many of the people from here."

"I see." From her comment he derived that she did not go out much in public and that she was not from this area. As for the latter point, it made sense that a local girl might find it difficult to be in this line of work if half the men who knocked on the door were relatives. To the extent that it mattered, he liked her being an outsider. "Do you come from very far?" he asked.

"From the Republic."

He took that to mean Mexico proper, as opposed to this northern frontier, as the people seemed to regard it. "Do you expect to go back?"

She smiled. "Maybe some day. I need to save my money to buy a business, like a restaurant or a store."

"I hope it goes well for you and that you may be successful in your country."

"Thank you. Have you ever been there?"

"No. I've seen pictures, nothing more."

"It is very nice. If you like to go to far places and see the sights, there are many

134

things there."

"A good idea."

She brushed her leg against his and met him with her soft, dark eyes. "And tonight?"

He felt his boldness rising. "The same as before? What do you think?"

"As you say, a good idea. If that's what you have in mind."

"The same way?"

"Yes, if you liked it."

"I was enchanted. For that reason my feet brought me back here."

She laughed as she rose from the couch and took his hand. "You are very nice. And you have smart feet."

In the room, she let him undress her as before. It was a little world unto itself where everything went well. He felt competent with his hands and the rest after that. When he lay beneath the cover a while later, admiring her loose dark hair on the pillow, he said, "It never occurred to me that my feet had any awareness, but you said they were smart."

"If they brought you back here. We'll see if they do it again."

"I hope so."

On his way to the inn, he savored the afterglow of his brief time with her. His senses were a swirl of bronze skin, tender touch, dark hair and eyes, and soft, flowing motion.

An image intruded of Carlos in his anguish, then another of young Ricardo Vega laid out in his best suit with his hands folded across his chest. Devon wondered if Ricardo had ever been to the parlor he had just left, or to some place like it. Probably so. It was too bad he would never know the pleasures of the world again, but life went on. As the old proverb said, not a plow stops when a man dies.

There would be time to think about that tomorrow. Devon brushed away the thoughts of sad young men and recalled again the warm interlude with Ramona. That was his good fortune for the moment, and he was going to enjoy it. If he got to do so again, so much the better.

CHAPTER SEVEN

Devon sat with his back against the wall that divided the priest's quarters from the main building of the church. Across the room in front of him, about twelve feet away, stood the stone fireplace. Except for a couple of gaps where rocks had fallen from the top of the opening, it was intact. Four feet to the left of it stood an open doorway looking out onto the plain. Like the other exterior doorways in the church ruins, this one had a barricade of rocks about three feet high.

The adobe that the door was set into was much thicker than the wooden frame, so the wall came out from the doorway nearly a foot and had been finished square all the way around. Like so many other spots he had seen here, the flat area of the wall showed various levels of deterioration. On the right-hand side, as with the doorway he had sketched a couple of days earlier, the bare ends of the adobe block showed through from about the height of the lintel to about the middle of the doorway. Back from that barest exposure lay an irregular area of adobe-colored mortar, covered in turn by a jagged layer of stucco-like plaster, which here and there, by the vagaries of time and weather, still held patches of paint.

As he sketched the scene, he wondered again if he would be able to capture his idea — in this instance, the degrees of resistance to time. Of that which was visible, the thinnest and least resistant was the paint, of course, but something that had an even shorter duration was the man, or series of men, who had lived in these quarters. Through that doorway the priest would have carried in firewood and hauled out ashes; he would have gone outside at times of necessity, and he no doubt would have paused there, now and then, to ponder the vast landscape. Devon feared that in the end he would have only a picture of cracked plaster and flaking paint, that he would not be able to imbue the scene with an idea about change or with the feeling that a person had once dwelt here.

He told himself he could not let himself worry about doing it all at once. He needed to work on it in parts; today was just a study. If he worked on all the little pieces, perhaps they would come together.

As he worked, he wondered if he would have any visitors today. News of Ricardo's death should have made its way to the ranch the day before, and certainly by this morning at the latest. He imagined that if anyone were to come by, it would be Don Felipe or Alfonso, to tell him to go back to town and stay out of the way for a day or two. He did not relish the prospect of a solitary meeting with Don Felipe, but he felt that he himself had been neutral enough that no one would see him as troublesome. He was just the artist, a maker of pictures.

Devon smiled as he turned his pencil sideways to shade the interior of the scene. Men's wives had run off with painters; their daughters had been seduced by them. For that matter, wives and daughters had been seduced by priests as well, perhaps even in this room. In the world at large, men and women had had their trysts in coaches and cloakrooms, woodsheds and haymows, law offices and graveyards. It was folly for a man to think he could screw down his control like a giant wine press, even if he had some good sense as to the parties he should leave alone.

The short, low sound of a human voice took

him out of his work and his wandering speculations. He rose from his seat on the floor and made his way through the main part of the church. He thought it a little too early for Petra to be visiting, but when he reached a window opening on the side where she had arrived before, there sat the horse and buggy with the aged driver in his usual relaxed pose. Petra sat in the shade of the canopy, her dark hair and light complexion visible.

Devon presented himself at the window and, touching his hat brim, called out, *"Buenos días."*

Petra called back the same, then spoke to Miguel, who climbed down from his seat to hand her to the ground.

She opened her parasol and walked toward the building in her airy way. Devon noticed that her hair was tied back as usual, and she had on a pair of dark red earrings the size of .45-caliber bullet points. She wore a dark jacket and white blouse, with the silver cross shining on her chest. Her dark skirt flared out and reached down to her ankles, covering the top buttons on her shoes. From her fresh and untroubled expression, Devon guessed she had not heard any upsetting news.

"How are you today?" she asked as she

came to a rest and gave him her gloved hand.

He caught a small trace of perfume as he took her hand and released it. "Well enough. And yourself?"

"Quite well." She turned her head to survey the building, as if he were working on the structure itself. "And how goes your work?"

"Rather well, I think. There are always new perspectives to gather, and little by little they may add up."

"Then you are not in a hurry to leave Rancho Agua Prieta?"

"Not unless someone is in a hurry for me to leave."

She gave a light laugh. "To the contrary. As I said before, my mother is very pleased that the rancho is worthy of an artist's attention."

"It is small homage when the artist's abilities are not very considerable."

She directed her tight smile at him as she tilted her head. "You are very modest."

He smiled, relaxed. "I try to tell the truth."

"Always the best." She looked at the ground and then at him again.

"What else?" he asked.

"Tell me, are you a prisoner of your work today?"

"Do you mean, am I governed by it?"

"Oh, no. I mean, can you leave? My mother would like to invite you to eat with us, but we do not want to interrupt your work."

Devon tried to catch a quick study of her face, but he found it impenetrable. "As I said, my work is in small pieces. There is no imperative schedule or sequence. And I greatly appreciate your mother's courtesy."

With a tiny smile she gave a nod of acknowledgment. "Did you not bring your own meal?"

"Oh, yes, but I'm sure it will keep for a day. It will be a pleasure to have dinner at your house."

"Excellent. It will please my mother."

"At about what time, then?"

"A little before one."

He gave a faint wag to his head. "I don't want to be a prisoner of the clock, of course."

She twirled her parasol. "Oh, that was a thoughtless thing for me to say, wasn't it? It was not well considered."

"Don't give it a thought. We are all prisoners to something, at one time or another. Better it should be work than some other things."

"That is true. My mother said you are intelligent, and she is right."

"I will try not to prove her wrong."

They both laughed.

Petra, with her voice raised a little, said, "We will expect you then." She gave him her hand and walked to the carriage. Miguel let himself down, handed her up to her seat beneath the canopy, and climbed back to his place. Petra waved her white gloved hand as the buggy turned, and the visit was over. As the vehicle rolled away, Devon scanned the surrounding plain to see if anyone had ridden out as a chaperone today. To his surprise, he saw no one.

The gate of Rancho Agua Prieta swung open as Devon drew near. The headquarters had a still, quiet appearance as he passed through the stone gateway. The leaves on the cottonwoods around the dark pool did not move; no horses were tied in the training area, and no people stirred. Devon expected Alfonso to come thundering in behind him, but no such thing happened. Except for a couple of horses thumping in their stalls, no sounds carried as he rode to the stone water trough, dismounted, loosened the cinch, and let his horse drink. Then he led the animal to the hitching rail and tied him.

He heard no sounds from within as he walked to the entryway of the *portal.* There he paused, still hearing nothing, until he took out his penknife and rapped on the frame of the walk-through door. After a long moment of waiting, the door opened to show Consuelo's anxious countenance.

"Yes, sir?"

"The señora and her daughter invited me."

"One minute, please."

She closed the door partway, and Devon heard footsteps on the paving stones. He did not hear anyone go into the house. Then he heard footsteps returning, and Consuelo opened the door again.

"Please come in." She stood back, smoothing her hands on her apron.

As Devon stepped into the roofed area of the *portal* and was letting his eyes adjust from the glare outside, Consuelo motioned with her left hand toward the patio.

"The señorita waits for you."

Devon saw her then as she rose from her chair. The table had been pulled closer in to the *portal,* as the shade had not yet stretched very far out to the patio. He crossed the paved area, noticing that the tack room on his right was closed.

"Buenas tardes," he called as he took off his hat.

She returned the greeting.

"I hope I'm not too early." He heard the door close as Consuelo went into the house.

"Not at all. Please sit down." She gave him her hand for a light touch and settled again onto her chair.

"It's a nice day," he said. "Warm, but very agreeable. Calm and quiet."

"Yes, that is nice."

"And your mother is well?"

She seemed to hesitate. "Well, yes. But there has been a small change in plans. Earlier in the day, before I went to invite you, she did not think that he was going to eat here at midday. But as it turns out, he does not leave."

Devon asked his question without thinking very far ahead. "Oh, did he change his mind when he found out that the two of you invited me?"

"I don't know," was her quick response. "Sometimes it is his way, to change things on short notice. But I don't ask him."

"Very well. I gather that they have the custom of taking their meal together, but by themselves."

"Something like that. But you are still invited, I assure you. If you don't mind, we

145

will eat out here."

"Enchanted."

"My mother will join us by and by, I am sure."

"Whenever she wishes, it will be a pleasure."

"Yes, and like you say, it is a very pleasant day."

At the sound of the house door opening, Devon turned in his seat. When he saw that it was only Consuelo, he wished he had had better repose — like Petra, who sat relaxed as she gazed across the patio at the now-fruitless plum and peach trees.

Consuelo spoke a few words in a low voice to Petra, got a *"sí"* for a response, and went back into the house.

"It is certainly quiet today," Devon resumed.

"Oh, yes."

"I don't mean to say this in a negative way, of course, but do you ever get bored?"

She widened her eyes and tilted her head. "Not much. And you?"

"Oh, no. I don't. I always have things to absorb my attention."

"My father always said it was not good to be bored. It made a person wish for life to pass by too quickly."

Devon realized it was the first time today

she had mentioned her father. As a more general reflection, he thought she wasn't very conversational yet, either. "I would agree with that. I'm sure your father had a great deal of wisdom."

"Oh, yes. He lived through many things, and they were not lost on him."

"I can see he was a good example for you."

Her look fell. "Sometimes I think I do not benefit enough." Then she seemed to get control of herself, for she raised her head and had an impassive expression on her face. "At other times, however, I think he would approve of some things as little as I do. Perhaps even less."

"It's difficult to say, isn't it?"

"He was a hard man at times. He had to be. I know he would understand why I don't conform. And as for other things, such as the habits I mentioned the other day, I have no doubt of what he would think."

"Yet things go on in their own way, don't they?"

She seemed to be looking down her nose at her own gloved hands, which she held together on the table in front of her. "So it seems." Then her eyes met his again as she said, "Why did you ask if I get bored? Do I look bored? Or does this life seem boring to you?"

"Neither of the two. It's just that people in town have told me that nothing ever happens here, and I was wondering how you saw it."

The corners of her mouth went down. "People say many things. It doesn't do to pay them much mind."

Consuelo came out with a large round tray. On it were two covered plates, two glasses of what looked like fruit-flavored water, and a linen cloth wrapped in the shape of a stack of tortillas. Petra sat with her hands in her lap as the servant rested the tray on the edge of the table and set the meal out.

"Un momento," said the older woman. She turned and hurried away, and a couple of minutes later she returned with napkins and silverware. *"Provecho,"* she said with a slight bow as she withdrew.

Petra raised the cover of her plate, and Devon did likewise. As the steam cleared, he saw the encouraging prospect of strips of meat that had been cooked with green chile, onion, and tomato. To the side of the main serving sat a mound of refried beans with a melted cap of white cheese.

"Here are the tortillas," said Petra, reaching into the cloth and taking out a corn tortilla for herself.

Devon did likewise, and the two of them ate without speaking. Consuelo appeared once, and at a word from Petra she went back to the house. Devon wondered if she was waiting on two tables at once or if the master had finished earlier and was now lingering over his second cigarette.

The silence continued for a while longer. Devon finished his meal and fruit drink and was beginning to think about dessert when he heard a commotion out front. At first it was a rumble of horse hooves, and as that noise faded, there came the sound of men's voices.

Petra looked at him with a questioning frown.

"Someone is here," he said. "Shall we go see?"

"Yes."

She rose from her seat as he did, and they walked together to the entry that was built into the large double door. Devon opened the smaller door inward to let Petra peer out.

"Do you know them?"

"Some of them."

"Shall we go outside?"

"Yes. There's nothing to worry about."

Petra stepped through the doorway and Devon followed, putting on his hat and then taking a place to her right as the men and horses milled in the dust that had risen. All of the riders had dismounted and were now gathering their reins and getting the horses settled. One man had handed his reins to another and was coming forward. He had a large gray mustache and a florid face that went along with his full girth. He wore a tall, dark brown hat, a wool vest of a lighter shade, a gray wool shirt, tan leather gloves, and a pistol with a dark brown grip. Devon counted the others. There were five, with the six horses.

"Good afternoon," said the man.

"Good afternoon, Sheriff," answered Petra. "In what way can we help you?"

After a glance at Devon, the man said, "Is your father at home?"

Petra's face stiffened. "You mean Don Felipe, of course. I believe he is within the house."

She turned to the open doorway, as did Devon, in time to see Consuelo going into the house.

A couple of minutes later, Don Felipe emerged in full dress, complete with his black sombrero and embroidered jacket, his pearl-gray shirt, his pistol and riding quirt, his trousers with the braided seams, and his boots and spurs. The large rowels clinked as he came out of the shaded *portal* and stood in the sunlight on the other side of Petra. Behind him in the doorway stood Emilia, looking worried and hesitant, and at her shoulder, just behind, stood Consuelo.

"Don Felipe," began the sheriff. *"Buenas tardes."*

"Muy buenas." Don Felipe's eyes traveled to the other men and back to the sheriff. "And how can I be of service to you today?"

"Regrettably, I have had to come to ask questions."

Don Felipe raised his chin and, with his left hand, lifted a tailor-made cigarette to his lips and took a puff. "Indeed?"

"Yes. About a very unfortunate thing that has happened." The sheriff's eyes were roving, as if he were reluctant to proceed.

"Good enough. Go ahead."

The sheriff held his gaze steadier. "You have known Ricardo Vega, I am sure."

"Without a doubt."

"And it is said that recently you had some strong words with him."

Don Felipe, with the advantage of standing on slightly higher ground than the sheriff, plus with his additional height, was able to look down on the man. "Nothing to be sorry for. I simply told him to stay away from my daughter."

The sheriff flicked a glance at Petra and came back to Don Felipe. "I understand that you told him to stay off your land, otherwise he risked his life."

Don Felipe made a dismissive expression. "These young men are headstrong, impulsive. I felt it necessary to use forceful words, to let him know I was serious, and that's why I don't regret it. He hasn't come back."

"But you did make the threat?"

"Of course I did. Why deny it? Several people heard it." He took another drag from the cigarette.

"Are you a man of your word?"

A look of disdain crossed over Don Felipe's face as he raised his right hand. After pointing at the sheriff he turned his finger to his own chest and said, "I, sir, am a horseman, skilled in my art and steeped in my honor. I am the master of this rancho, which you are now on. I do not toss around my words in vain. And I believe this young Ricardo Vega knows it, and for that he has not come back but rather goes crying to you."

The man of the law showed a stirring of dignity himself. "It is well that you have such a high opinion of yourself, but I did not come to chide you for your threat."

With his free right hand, Don Felipe

waved toward the other men. "Then why do you all take the trouble to come here?"

"Because," said the sheriff, "the young man Ricardo Vega is no longer alive."

Devon, who had been waiting for this moment of disclosure, took a close glance at the people to his left. Petra made no expression at all, while Don Felipe raised his cigarette, flicked his ash, and took a drag. In back of him, Doña Emilia's look of worry had transformed into one of shock.

The sheriff put back his shoulders and said, "He was found, shot, on his father's land."

Don Felipe sniffed. "Better there than here. Perhaps that explains why he didn't come back."

"You don't seem very concerned."

The master of the rancho gave a quick frown, shadowed by the brim of his large sombrero. "It's not for me to look after him. I told him to stay away, and he did. Beyond that, I can't let myself worry very much."

"You seem to be certain of the sequence."

"How is that?"

"That he died before he ever came back here."

Don Felipe held out both hands, palm up, with smoke curling into view on the left. "What else can I assume?"

"Others have their own ideas."

"I'm sure they do."

"Those of Ricardo's family, his father and his brothers, want an investigation."

"As well they should." Don Felipe lifted his cigarette.

"They say Ricardo left their rancho on Saturday night, and although he did not declare it directly to them, it was understood among them and the hired men that he was coming here, for the señorita Petra." Then, turning to her, the sheriff said, "With my respect."

"Proper," said Petra.

"Bah!" Don Felipe blew out a puff of smoke. "I don't believe he had the *pantalones* for it."

"With my respect to you, sir, this was his understood destination, and he was found dead. His father and his brothers want to find out why."

"Well enough. And is this the only possibility? Is there no one else who could have done it? Why hang all of your ropes on a single peg?"

"There is a history of hostility here."

"As there may well be elsewhere. Have you not considered anyone else?"

The sheriff gave an open look. "In truth, we have. One Carlos Hernández, cousin and hopeful suitor of the señorita — with your permission — is known to have been jealous."

"Well, perhaps it would be fitting that you go and subject him to an interrogation — in front of his family, as you have done here. I, for one, do not take it lightly. There is very little that a man can take with him to his grave, but one thing is his honor."

"And on yours, you did not cause the death of Ricardo Vega?"

"If he did not come here, I did not have a reason to lift a finger."

"Very well," said the sheriff, but he did not move. After a few seconds he continued. "It is not impossible that he came, that something happened to him, and that he was carried back to his father's ranch."

"More likely that someone got to him there. These young men are very impetuous."

"Nevertheless, if there is no objection, I would like to ask the *señorita* a question or two."

Don Felipe gave a backhand wave. "She is old enough."

The sheriff turned to Petra. "Very well, señorita. I am sorry to ask indiscreet questions, but as you understand, the family of the young man wishes to learn the truth."

"All very proper." Petra lifted her eyebrows in an open expression.

"Well, then. First, do you think Ricardo Vega had an intention of coming here?"

"I did think that, yes."

"On the basis of — ?"

"He said he would come."

The sheriff nodded. "That's what we've heard. And when did you expect him to come?"

"Saturday. The night before last."

Devon stole a glance at Don Felipe, who was running the tip of his tongue along his lip beneath his mustache.

"Did you wait up for him?"

"Yes."

"And what happened?"

Don Felipe had his head up and the last inch of his cigarette raised to his lips. For that instant Devon saw the practiced poise of a man facing the firing squad.

After a couple of seconds of silence, Petra's voice came out clear and steady. "Nothing."

"Nothing happened? How long did you stay up?"

"Until long after midnight. I stayed up and listened. He was going to whistle." She turned her head less than an inch, a motion made noticeable as her bright red earring caught the sun.

"And you heard nothing? No one coming or going?"

Petra's face was unwavering, and it seemed to Devon that she was looking past the sheriff in the direction of the dark pool and the cottonwood trees. "Nothing," she said. "Ricardo never came."

CHAPTER EIGHT

Back at his study at the old church, Devon pondered the texture of adobe in the afternoon shade. It was a good, small thing to focus on as he tried to make sense of what he had seen of Petra today. If she had not heard of Ricardo's death before the sheriff announced it, she had very little emotion to show. If she had known already, either she had done a good job of concealing her knowledge in her two conversations with Devon, or the death had had little effect on her. In any case, it did not seem as if she had much sympathy, much less romantic ardor, for Ricardo. It was hard to know, then, what to make of her admitted willingness to run away with him. It may have been more talk than real intention, to spite her stepfather and her mother as well. She showed no discomfort at admitting to it, but there was no telling what she would have done if the moment had come for action.

Her admission itself, in retrospect, seemed almost too matter-of-fact, as if she had not expected Ricardo to begin with and had not waited up for him. Perhaps she had, even if she was not that enthralled with him, and then when he failed to show, she shrugged it off. Then again, she might have received a message that he would come, then gone to bed early and had her sweet head resting in slumber on a soft pillow, as Carlos would have liked to imagine it, and heard nothing whether Ricardo came or not. But it was difficult to think she would lie about expecting him to come, and it was at least as improbable that she would have heard or seen something and then lied to protect Don Felipe.

Something was missing, he was sure of that. If it wasn't in Petra's account of things, which held together almost too well, in view of her lack of enthusiasm or feeling for Ricardo, it was in the actual sequence of events. If Ricardo did not come to the rancho, how did he meet his death? Devon could not envision Carlos going out to challenge him, or even winning if he ventured that far, and he could not picture Don Felipe coming and going without being heard. That left the possibility of a third suspect.

One would think of Alfonso, but he had been at the rooster fight and then in the cantina. Beyond that, Devon had no idea what other suspects might be out there.

Even if someone else had waylaid Ricardo when he was on his way to the rancho, there was still something missing on this end of things. No matter how he kept mulling things over, Devon kept coming back to Petra. With all of her sense of propriety, would she really have run off with Ricardo? Would she have exposed herself to condescension from her stepfather, someone she considered to be lower in dignity than herself? Even if she wanted to spite him with her admission, wouldn't it give him something to hold over her? One would think so, yet she was as undaunted as a stone.

All the time that Devon sketched the exposed adobe blocks and worked on the puzzle, he listened for the sound of the buggy. He doubted she would come. Only a couple of hours had passed since he had left in the wake of the sheriff's visit, and though he and Petra had agreed to continue the visit again before long, he expected she would wait at least until the next day before she sallied out again in full repose.

Presently he had the sense that he had been hearing a sound and was just now becoming aware of it. It was a low, uneven, muffled sound of movement, with an occasional tinkling. He went to the side of the church opposite from where Petra arrived, and as he looked through a window opening, he saw a herd of sheep about three hundred yards away. Now he could hear their hooves crunching on the dry grass and scuffing on the earth. The animals were moving to his left, with a man on foot in back and a dog circling around this side. The man was leading a pack burro and carrying a shepherd's staff. Devon stood at the window, and when the sheepherder came opposite and waved, he waved back.

The air was dry and hazy already, and now the dust of a thousand hooves hung like a thin cloud. The combination of dust and sheep smell reached Devon where he stood and looked out. The sheepherder walked to the far side of the bunch, then came back in Devon's direction. He waved again, turned and walked along the flank of the herd for about forty yards, and then left the herd and came toward the church with his staff in his hand. The burro trailed behind on a lead rope.

When he was within thirty yards, the man called out, *"Buenas tardes."*

Devon returned the greeting and observed

the man as he came closer. He was of average height and slender, wearing a straw hat, drab peasant clothes, and leather sandals.

Smiling, he called out, "How are you?"

Devon noted the use of the formal *usted* form and used the same form in his answer. "Fine, and yourself?"

"Well enough." After a pause, the man asked, "Are you the artist?"

"Yes, I am."

"That's what I thought. They said there was an American artist here, doing pictures of the *tapias*."

Devon smiled and squinted into the sun as he nodded.

"Say," said the man. "Do you have the makings of a cigarette?"

"No, I don't. Sorry."

"Oh, that's all right. It's good to come and say hello anyway."

"Yes, it is."

The man lingered, as if he was trying to think of something to say. "Are you here for very long?"

"This is my third day out here. I'm staying in town. Maybe a week longer."

"That's good."

"And yourself, you take care of sheep?"

"Yes."

"For the rancho?"

"Yes, Rancho Agua Prieta."

"Good work, I hope."

"Good enough."

"I've met Alfonso. I suppose you deal mostly with him."

"Alfonso, yes."

Devon wondered how much more conversation he could make. He recalled Carlos's comment that a common peon wouldn't be allowed a horse. "Is that your burro?"

"Yes."

"Is it a good one? What's its name?"

"Perla." Pearl.

"That's a nice name." Devon saw that the dog, a medium-sized black-and-white animal, had come up and was standing in the burro's shadow. "Good dog."

"Yes, he's a good one."

"A good dog is a treasure for a sheepherder, isn't it?"

"Oh, yes."

"Do you always have just one?"

"No, sometimes I have two, or three. I had another one, but it got killed."

"Some bad luck."

"I suppose. The *patrón* killed him."

Devon made a face. "That's too bad."

"The dog came too close to the *patrón's* horse, so he took out his pistol and gave it to him."

"I'm sorry."

"Oh, there's not much to be done about it. We do our work and try to be happy."

"Alfonso understands better."

"Maybe." The man didn't say anything for a moment as he glanced around at the walls of the church. "Are you going to do a big painting?"

"Probably a few small or medium ones."

"That's good." He turned and looked at his burro, and the dog perked up.

"I'm sorry I don't have any tobacco."

"Oh, that's all right. It was worth asking. And I'm glad to meet you."

"The same."

The man stepped forward as Devon leaned out, and they shook hands. Then with a flick of the lead rope, the sheepherder turned and headed back to his flock. The dog, light-footed, went at his side.

Nice enough fellow. Probably didn't have many choices in life, though. And he probably didn't get much tobacco from Alfonso.

Devon went back to his sketch and tried to concentrate, but his thoughts returned to Petra. Try as he might to make sense of her attitude toward Ricardo, she remained inscrutable. On a smaller scale, he didn't know what to make of her interest in him — whether she saw him as a curiosity, as something potentially more affectionate, or just a convenient burr to put under Don Felipe's saddle.

With the various interruptions that had come his way, he felt he hadn't made much progress, so he decided to call it quits for the day. He packed up his pencils and sketch pad and got the horse ready to go. Rather than cut straight across the plain to strike the road that led from the headquarters back to town, he meandered in the direction of the rancho. He admitted to himself that he had no clear objective — he was hoping he might cross paths with Petra, but he didn't think he would go through the stone gateway and ask for her. Rather, if he bumped into someone, either Alfonso or a lesser hand, he might ask if he could go in and water his horse. If he saw no one, he could wander back to the road and return to town.

He loafed along, then, with his feet light in the stirrups and his upper body rocking with the movement of his horse. Now and then he cast his glance at the plains around him. It would be a while until the rancho came into view. He studied the ground for a while, wondering from what direction the sheep had come. The grass here was short and dry, but it hadn't been grazed close or trampled.

When he looked up again, he felt a small jolt in the pit of his stomach and then made the identification. Ahead of him on the plain, half a mile away, appeared a white horse with a rider in black. The horse came straight at him, then turned almost ninety degrees and gave a partial profile of the right side. The horse seemed to sidestep for a few paces until it straightened out again. A hundred yards closer, it turned again and stepped as before. Then it turned and gave a left-side view and came prancing from that angle. After several minutes of display, the horse fell into a normal path again and came forward at a brisk walk, lifting its feet in sharp strokes and causing the black sombrero to move up and down.

Devon kept his own mount on its casual forward course. He felt silly, not because of his own plodding progress but because of the contrast between his plain presence and the elaborate self-presentation of the master of the rancho.

When Don Felipe drew up alongside, Devon noticed not only the customary clothing but also a pair of dark gray riding gloves. From there he took in the braided reins, horsehair noseband, and laced leather headstall with silver conchos.

"Buenas tardes," he said.

"Buenas." The master drew rein so that his right hand was poised about a foot above and forward from his pistol grip. The riding quirt dangled from his wrist. He had his chin lifted so that the wide sombrero brim made a dark circle against the sky. "Do you look for something?" he asked.

"No, not really."

"If it's not much trouble, could you tell me where you're headed?"

Devon shrugged. "To town, I assume. I've done my study for the day."

"That's fine. Perhaps you are aware that the town is more in that direction." He showed his teeth as he motioned with his head.

"Yes, but when I go this way, I am sure I can find the road."

Don Felipe looked him up and down. "It's easy to get lost farther out on the *llano,* but here, the road can be found from anywhere."

"Yes, and I know there are even paths I can follow to get there, just as when I come from town. But a herd of sheep came through, and the ground doesn't look the same."

"Sheep."

"Yes, a herd of them. Yours, I believe."

"No doubt." Don Felipe squinted as he looked out upon the plain. Then his nostrils flared, and his gaze came back to Devon. "Look," he said, using the formal mode of address as always, "it's all right for you to come and draw your pictures. But do not go seeking other things."

"Very well. I —"

"Understood?"

"Yes, understood."

"Good enough." The master seemed to settle down an inch. "Have a safe trip to town. And may you continue to find inspiration in our humble church."

"Thank you."

"De nada," he said in a curt tone, with his mouth open and his lower teeth showing. He turned his horse toward the rancho, put it into a trot for twenty yards, and then spurred it to a gallop.

Devon watched the black-and-white figure recede. He didn't think the master had lost much self-assurance through the visit from the sheriff, but he wondered if this most recent gesture came from a need to reassert his authority. It could be. Petra's statement that she had planned to run off with Ricardo may have stirred the stepfather's pot enough to compel him to take it out on the nearest possible suitor.

Still, he was the landowner, and he had made clear what the artist was welcome to do. Devon turned his horse to the left and headed north, telling himself he needed to respect the bounds of hospitality and at the same time admitting he had let the other man play out his role as the dominant male. It was like one dog covering another's mark, or a horse laying back his ears and getting ready to take a gouge out of an animal lower in the pecking order. Devon didn't like the feeling, and he knew he was going to have to learn to summon up resistance.

In town, he let the horse drink at the stone water tank as he lifted his hat and dragged his shirtsleeve across his forehead. He felt as if he had put in a full day's work, but in the view of a blacksmith or even a sheepherder, it was trivial play. So be it. At least he knew what he was working on, or he thought he did.

When the horse pulled his dripping muzzle up from the tank, Devon led him back to the stable and turned him in. From there he carried his duffel bag to the inn and mounted the stairs to his room, where he took off his boots and stretched out on the bed to rest.

He had put his boots on and was cleaning

up for the evening meal when he heard a knock on the door. Crossing the room, he opened the door and met the dark features of the innkeeper, who had given him the room key a short while before. The man handed him a folded piece of paper, made a half-bow, and turned away. Devon unfolded the sheet of paper and read, in a clear hand, an invitation from Carlos Hernández to come and take the evening meal at his house.

Devon finished getting cleaned up and read the note again to be sure. Then he went downstairs, turned in his key, and told the landlord he had an invitation to dine elsewhere.

The long shadows of evening lay on the town as Devon made his way to the Hernández residence. He tapped on the front gate with his penknife, and in less than a minute his friend came stepping out of the house to invite him in. The man was dressed in his brown corduroy, and he seemed to have regained his composure. He was clear-eyed and clean-shaven, and his grip was firm as he shook Devon's hand and thanked him for coming.

With the preliminary greeting taken care of, Carlos led him around the side of the house to sit at the table where they had sat the evening before. A wine bottle and two glasses stood ready.

"Let's sit down," said the host.

"Thank you."

When they were seated, Carlos lifted the bottle and pointed it at Devon's glass. "Do you care for some?"

"Certainly."

Carlos poured dark red wine into Devon's glass and then his own, filling each one halfway. *"Salud,"* he said, raising his glass to touch his guest's.

"Salud."

After a respectful pause to sip the wine, Carlos spoke. "And how are things for you today? Were you able to continue your artistic study?"

Devon pressed his tongue against his palate, rubbing at the dry, almost bitter taste of the wine. "Yes, I was. There is always something new to see."

"Such a good thing, to have a purpose and to dedicate oneself."

"It probably does not seem important to some people, but it holds my interest at the present."

"It is your work."

"You make it sound so big, and it is my work, at least in part. All the same, to me this study seems like such a small thing,

171

and I must confess it is not a major project in a full profession. I have really not arrived at that stage yet."

"Oh, but you are young, and it's not good to worry too much about the future."

"Yes, but I feel that I have to do something, at some time, and meanwhile the years pass by."

Carlos made a face, half frown and half smile. "Does it proceed from your national character, this obsession to acquire and achieve?"

Devon laughed. "I suppose it has some effect. I feel that I should do something, and furthermore I would not be satisfied if it were something common, though I fear that's how I might end up."

"Such fears." Carlos reached into his coat pocket, took out a cigarette case, and offered Devon a tailor-made cigarette.

"No, thanks."

Carlos struck a match and lit a cigarette for himself.

"I'll tell you," Devon continued. "I saw a man today who left me with something to think about. He was a sheepherder, working for Rancho Agua Prieta. He was moving sheep past the old church, and he stopped to say hello. Now, he's a man with work to do, always busy from the looks of it, and I imagine he has found a way to be happy with what he does. At least he said so to me. I know that his life is important to him, as much as mine is to me, and I respect how he spends his time. Yet I would not be satisfied if I worked at that level all my life."

Carlos blew out a breath of smoke. "But you won't."

"I don't know that. If I cannot distinguish myself in some small way at least, I may settle to a level of common work and be just another face on the street, someone who will not be missed."

After another sip of wine, Carlos gave a toss of the head. "Don't be so pessimistic. Maybe you'll marry a rich woman, and she'll be happy to have an artist beneath her roof."

Devon laughed. "I met a man like that today, too."

"Oh, really?"

"Actually, I met him before, but I met up with him today. Don Felipe."

"Oh, him. You have him as an artist?"

"Somewhat by his own declaration. I understand that he sees his horsemanship as his art."

"Perhaps so." Carlos lapsed into a pensive mode. "So you saw him today? And the others?"

"Yes, I had the good fortune to see your cousin. She invited me, on behalf of her mother, to come to the rancho to eat at midday, but things did not turn out perfect. Doña Emilia was obliged to eat inside with her husband."

Carlos smiled. "Ah, yes. My cousin does not take meals with him."

Devon assumed Carlos had invited him in order to learn whatever Devon had picked up today, so he went ahead. "And then the dinner was cut short, as was the visit, by the arrival of the sheriff."

"Bonifacio?"

"I suppose."

"And what did he say?" Carlos affected a tolerant look as he blew out another stream of smoke.

"Oh, the expected. That Ricardo had been found dead, and that he was thought to be going to the rancho."

"And what did Don Felipe say?"

"He took the high-handed approach, saying that yes, he had warned Ricardo but the young man didn't have the *pantalones* to come back, and he, as a man of honor and practitioner of his art, did not like to have it suggested that he did anything other than to stand ready to keep his own word."

"In other words, he denied doing it."

174

"He denied all possibilities, except that someone else must have done it."

"Meaning me."

"That seemed to be the second option."

Carlos shook his head, and any humor he had summoned up was now gone. "Oh, my God. And what did my cousin say?"

Devon grimaced. "It displeases me to tell you that part, but I feel I must."

Carlos waved his hand as he drank from his glass. "Oh, yes, yes. This is all in confidence. Drink some more of your wine."

"Good enough." Devon took a drink and went on. "She says, and I repeat that she says this, however sincerely she may mean it, that she was planning to leave with Ricardo, that she waited up for him, and that he never came."

Carlos gave a curious look. "Really? She said that? In front of him, her stepfather?"

"Yes. I don't know if she said it to sting him, but the result was that it allowed him to continue to insist that he had done nothing and that the sheriff should look somewhere else."

Now Carlos stared wide-eyed. "Me."

Devon shrugged. "So it seems."

"Oh, this is no good. Not at all." Carlos shook his head and stared at the table. Then he looked up. "And what did my cousin seem to think of me when they said this?"

"She didn't give any indication."

"She didn't care, did she?"

"I don't know. Curiously, she didn't seem to care about any of it. Not about Ricardo, whether he came, or that he was dead."

"She thinks I did it."

"I doubt it, but I don't know."

"And the sheriff?"

"I don't know that, either, but I thought he gave up too easily at the end. When Don Felipe talked down to him, he got proud in return, but when Petra said Ricardo never came, it seemed to take the wind out of his sails, at least for the time being."

Carlos still shook his head. "He thinks I did it."

"I think he was forced to fall back on that option. Has he come to talk with you?"

"This morning."

"Did he seem to suspect you then?"

Carlos shrugged. "Not so much. He asked his questions, and he explained that he had to do this for Ricardo's family, that they insisted. He said that certain things did not look good for me, but he had yet to follow up with another party."

"Don Felipe."

"One assumed, though he didn't say the name. I felt, however, that he was not anxious to go there."

"Did he come here by himself?"

"Yes."

"Huh. He had a group of five others with him when he went to the rancho. It must have taken him a while to get them together."

"Probably." Carlos's tone was dejected. "And then they got turned away."

"One could say that."

Carlos let out a heavy sigh and crushed his cigarette, still half-smoked, in a clay dish that served as an ashtray. Then he took a drink of wine. "Oh, he'll be back, then. It's just a matter of time until I am formally accused, convicted, and punished — by death or by prison. There's no hope."

"Oh, don't give up so easily."

"What should I care, especially if she thinks I did it?"

"She hasn't said that, and I don't believe she does."

"They all do. Probably even my aunt. And the sheriff, if he believes it, he will find the proof. Easier than taking on Don Felipe. I haven't got a chance."

"Don't be such a fatalist."

"When the others have power and money, they don't lose."

"Look. You need to take more initiative,

not roll over and take a beating like a dog."

"That's an easy thing for you to say, but it is difficult to take action when a person knows everything is turned against him."

"You don't know that."

"Not yet, but I know some things. My uncle Vicente, for example, in his life, he never lost a case. The judges were his friends, and the lawyers, and this same sheriff Bonifacio."

"Did he ever commit a crime and put the blame on someone else?"

Carlos gave a surprised look. "Not that I know. But he went to court many times, and he always won. The ones who lost, they had no recourse. They had to find other land, other work, other places to live. Meanwhile my uncle accumulated property and had the law on his side."

"But Don Felipe is not the same. I doubt that he has the same friends."

"No, but he is still Rancho Agua Prieta, and that counts for a great deal. And besides, he has no reason to go easy on me. Quite to the contrary. If one way of maintaining his innocence is by heaping the blame on me, he will do it with pleasure."

"He will certainly try, but you have to do something to defend yourself, not just accept it."

"Like what?"

Devon paused. "I don't know."

"You see?" Carlos tossed off his remaining half-glass of wine and reached for the bottle. "What's the use?"

"It's worth trying. I still think something is not right at the rancho. I'll see what I can find out."

"At least you can go there. I can't even go to talk to my aunt."

Devon raised his eyebrows. "Don Felipe does not leave all the gates open for me, either. But if Petra drops by when I am at my work, as she has done, I may learn something that will help."

Devon stood at the bar in La Sombra. The beer tasted good after the salty meal of beans and fried pork chops at Carlos's house. He had drunk only his first half-glass of wine and had left the rest to his host, so he was ready for a couple of glasses of beer to knock the edges off.

The cantina had its regular small crowd of patrons. Devon had barely enjoyed his second sip of beer when Cayetano's long face appeared on his left.

"Buenas noches, jefe."

"Buenas noches."

"Do you look for your friend Carlos? I

think he is at home."

"I believe he is. I just saw him there."

"Very good. I did not expect to know more than you do."

"It would not be difficult."

"Oh, no. You are a man who goes into the world and knows people, while I am but a common laborer."

Devon gave a tiny shrug.

"For example, you go every day to Rancho Agua Prieta, do you not? There is much to be learned there, as well as with the good families here in town."

"You flatter me. I know nothing, I assure you."

Cayetano made a smile that verged on a leer. "I am sure everyone at the rancho is talking about Ricardo, who went out and got himself killed like a dog in the henhouse."

"They may speak of it, but not to me. Today I spoke with the graceful señorita, a passing sheepherder, and Don Felipe himself, and no one mentioned it to me."

Cayetano drew his mouth downward, then relaxed it. "For a small cooperation, I could tell you what everyone at the rancho seems to keep from you." He turned his head and gave a sidelong glance. "Or do you know everything, and you do not want to say?"

"I don't know anything."

"Well, if you did, you could share it with your friend Carlos. He does not come out of the house for two days, and Doña Flora does not let anyone in."

Devon felt disgusted with himself as he did it, but all the same he drew out a ten-cent piece and dropped it into Cayetano's palm.

"Muchas gracias, jefe. Que Dios le bendiga." May God bless you. With that benediction, Cayetano made good on his offer. "Here is what they say at the rancho. The señorita Petra was waiting for Ricardo. He was supposed to come on Saturday night, at midnight, like I told you. He was going to whistle to let her know he was there. She waited up, but he did not come. Don Felipe was also waiting, smoking a cigarette and drinking a *copita* of tequila as he put oil on the cylinder of his pistol, but Ricardo was a great poltroon. He did not come, but rather got himself killed before he left his own rancho."

"So who is the guilty one?"

"Suspicion falls on your friend Carlos, and although he is not very probable, he makes it worse for himself by hiding in his house."

Devon smiled. "People are very unkind to Carlos. He does not come out of his house because he has a large boil on the end of his nose."

"I did not see it when I took you there yesterday."

"Yes, and I did not hear Don Felipe tell about oiling his pistol when he and the gracious señorita were answering the sheriff's questions."

Cayetano's face broke into a smile. "So you do know everything."

"No, I don't. Who is the guilty one?"

Cayetano shrugged. "Who can say?"

"Some people are saying something. What is it?"

The long-faced man looked to either side before he shrugged and spoke again, this time in a lower voice. "Everyone knows Don Felipe is capable, but there is no proof. As to why, you already know, if you were there when the sheriff arrived." Cayetano gave him a shrewd look. "Were you, or did you repeat what someone told you?"

"Ask any of the five men who rode with the sheriff."

Cayetano laughed. "Very well, *jefe*. And thank you for your generosity. If I hear something else, I will tell you."

For a small price, of course. Devon took a drink of beer as the man moved away.

The rest of the sounds of the cantina came

182

to him again. Lalo the bartender was telling a joke about a cross-eyed burro, and Juanito was singing a song. It was a *corrido,* a tragic ballad, about a young man who got drilled with bullet holes as he went in the moonlight to carry away his young lady. No one knew the name of the killer, but the young man's soul turned into a pigeon and flew to the bell tower in the church of the town. And on some future Sunday, when the people least expected, a pigeon would sing out the murderer's name.

Cu-ru-cu, cu-ru-cu-cu, so sings the sad
   lover,
Who died in the moonlight surprised and
   alone.
Cu-ru-cu, cu-ru-cu-cu, so sings the lone
   pigeon,
Who waits for the day when the truth will
   be known.

Devon looked around at the other men in the cantina. Most of them were listening to Lalo's jokes, but a couple of them, including Alfonso, were listening to Juanito's *corrido.* The foreman was dressed as usual, with his cream-colored hat and brown leather vest, and he held a cornhusk cigarette in his hand at chest height. He was nodding his head to the rhythm, and his silver tooth showed in his smile.

CHAPTER NINE

Alone again at the church ruins, Devon studied the landscape as it was framed by a window arch. Far to the southwest, across a broad stretch of plain, a range of grayish-purple mountains stood out in the morning sun. He had no idea how far away they were — a two- or three-day ride, he supposed. On the *llano* that lay between, there were no doubt fences, watercourses, huts, ranch buildings, and even trees, all obscured by gentle undulations in the land, but from this distance he could see nothing but flat, empty country. It looked flatter than it was. He knew that much from his movements between the town, the church, and the rancho. A person thought he could see a great deal more than he could.

Relaxing his gaze, he glanced around the immediate interior of the church. He paused, noticing a dead snake he had seen earlier. It looked as if its head had been crushed by a rock and then some good-humored passerby, like Alfonso, had tossed the body through the window for his benefit. The snake was over a yard long, not huge and thick, but big enough to give a person a start the first time he saw it. Devon didn't care to touch snakes, but he knew he was going to have to get rid of this one before it developed a dead smell and became a haven for maggots.

After climbing through the window and landing outside, he wandered around on the grassland until he found a clump of brush, probably greasewood. With his foot he broke off a dead forking branch at the base. Then he stripped and snapped away pieces until one side of the fork was a handle and the other was a V-hook. With his primitive tool he went back to the church, climbed in, lifted the dead snake, and let it fall on the ground outside. Climbing out again, he hooked the snake and, holding it away from him so he wouldn't hit it with his leg, he carried it a couple of hundred yards out in the pastureland and gave it a fling. It landed in the trampled earth where the sheep had passed the day before. Well enough. Now the scavengers could have at it as they wished.

Back at his study, he returned to wondering whether Petra would show up today. Alternating with that hopeful thought was the worry that Don Felipe might come by and, still transferring his jealousy to any possible *pretendiente,* might be less hospitable than before. By now Alfonso would have learned that Devon was continuing his friendship with Carlos, and if he passed that information on to Don Felipe, the master might decide, on a whim, that he didn't need to patronize the arts anymore.

At mid-morning, shortly after Devon noticed the first two ravens settling down where he had left the snake, he heard the clop of hooves and the creak of the buggy. Going to the window on the opposite side, he saw Petra once again beneath the canopy of the carriage. He hiked himself up and over the window ledge to meet her.

Gray-haired Miguel remained in his seat, so Devon walked over to the buggy. *"Buenos días,"* he said.

"Buenos días," she answered. "I do not want to take up much of your time this morning, when you are so engaged in your work."

Devon noted how she phrased it this time. "Not at all," he said.

"But my mother and I are sorry not to have a complete meal or a satisfactory visit yesterday, and we would like to invite you to come again today, if you can accept."

"Will it not displease the master of the rancho?"

She made a light puffing sound, then said, "My mother has expressed her displeasure at not being able to receive you properly yesterday, as well as her wish to make amends today."

"I appreciate that. However, he gave me to understand yesterday afternoon that I was welcome principally to pursue my interests here at the church."

She made the dismissive *puh* sound again. "Have no worry. You will be welcome, as always, if you choose to accept."

"Of course I do. It is very gracious and kind."

Her eyes flashed in the interior of the buggy. Then she leaned forward, showing yet another pair of hard, glossy red earrings. She held forth her gloved hand. "You are the kind one," she said, "to change your schedule two days in a row, especially in view of the unpleasant scene yesterday."

He smiled as he took her hand and released it. "I think very little of it, as it was so long ago."

She gave a light laugh. "Thank you. My mother will be happy to know we can expect you." She sat back in her seat.

Devon stepped aside and watched as the buggy turned and rolled away, lifting wisps of dust and fragments of dry grass. She was a plucky one, all right.

As Devon approached the stone gateway of Rancho Agua Prieta, the most prominent features presented themselves now as familiar sights. The dark pool on his left appeared to be resting in the shade of the cottonwoods, and the long, low roof of the stables looked solid and timeless. A hired man emerged from the small-leafed trees behind the stone wall on the right and swung the gate inward. Devon touched his hat as he rode past.

All along the row of stables, horses came to the open upper doors and looked out. A couple of them neighed. Ahead on the left, the snubbing post stood unoccupied again, and around closer on the left, no movement appeared outside the bunkhouse or the blacksmith shop. At the other end of the parade ground, the doors to the carriage room and the tack room were both closed, as were the double doors to the *portal*. Devon rode his horse to the stone water trough, where he dismounted as usual, loosened the cinch, and let the animal drink.

As had happened on his first visit, he thought he heard a peacock cry. He had not seen any of the birds — not on the roof of the buildings, where they might like to perch, and not strutting around in the yard — nor had he seen feathers or droppings anywhere. Furthermore, he had the general sense that peacocks cried more in the mornings and evenings than at midday, which made him think it might be some other sound he heard, but he did not dismiss the possibility that one or more lived at the rancho.

He tied the horse at the hitching rail and knocked on the doorway that was set into the *portón,* or large door. Expecting to be met by Consuelo, he was surprised when the door opened upon the younger and radiant Petra.

"Come in," she said, opening the door further and standing back. She was wearing a dark blue dress, open at the throat, and he could see the top of her silver cross.

"Thank you." Devon took off his hat and passed through the doorway.

"The weather is not too hot yet?"

"Just a little," he said, fanning himself once with the hat.

She led the way to the entry to the house. "Come along," she said. "It is cooler inside."

Raising his eyebrows, he followed.

Inside, he and Petra waited on a slate entryway area as Doña Emilia rose from a couch and came toward them, her hands in front of her at waist level in an open gesture.

"How nice of you to come, señor *artista*," she said, with her soft brown eyes meeting his.

"The pleasure is mine." He touched both her hands and let go.

"Let us sit down." She swept her hand toward two couches and an armchair. "Dinner will be soon."

Consuelo emerged from behind the lady and took Devon's hat. He glanced around and chose a seat at the end of a leather couch. Petra and her mother sat on the other, facing him.

He smiled and looked around. The main walls of the house were of thick adobe, which accounted for the cooler temperature, and the interior structure was done in heavy posts and beams. At the end of the other couch, a square post rose up from a trapezoidal base for about seven feet. At its top, another trapezoidal figure, longer than the one below, sat long-side-up as it rested on the post like a capital. Running lengthwise with it and overlapping on it in over-and-under notches were two square beams about six inches by eight. Upon the main beams lay a series of crossbeams, and upon them lay close-fitted, varnished planks.

Lowering his gaze, he met the pleasant expression of Doña Emilia. Her dark hair was combed back and ridged up as before, and her neat hairline made a pretty contrast with her pale complexion. She was dressed again in a white blouse, black jacket, and dark skirt, and when she smiled, Devon appreciated her white, even teeth. Her face seemed relaxed, with less of the haunted look he thought he had seen before.

"And how does your art progress?" she asked.

"Well enough, I believe. I do things in parts or pieces, rather than try to do one large work in its entirety. Later, I will see how to put things together."

"It can be seen that you know your art and how to practice it."

"I cannot predict that it will be any good at all."

Petra spoke up. "The artist is very modest, mama. Always. My father would hold him in esteem, don't you think?"

Emilia showed a trace of pain as she smiled. "I'm sure."

"Excuse me for changing the subject,"

said Devon. "But it seemed to me that I heard the cry of a peacock when I was outside. But I have not seen any of the birds. Are there some?"

The lady's kind expression resumed. "Miguel keeps a few of them in a large cage. Out back, near the orchard. I think he has three. There used to be more, but Felipe doesn't like them very much, so he has them penned up."

Consuelo appeared from an adjoining room and announced that dinner was ready. Devon arose and followed the two ladies. In the dining room a long dark table was flanked by two high-backed chairs on each side and one at each end. Petra sat at the far end and indicated for Devon to sit at the side on her right. Emilia sat opposite him. Devon looked at the other place setting and wondered if Petra had deigned to sit at the same table as Don Felipe. Then he looked at mother and daughter, who were both smiling.

A minute later, Devon heard the heavy fall of boot heels and the clinking of spurs. Don Felipe appeared in the doorway, dressed in his embroidered black outfit and still wearing his pistol and his wide-brimmed sombrero.

Devon rose to say hello.

"Sit down," said the master, using the formal mode as always, for courtesy. He took off his hat and hung it on the knob of the chair that sat between Devon's place and his.

Emilia turned her smile toward her husband. "It is so good that the artist is able to join us today."

"Oh, yes."

"And also," she continued, smiling now at Petra and then at Devon, "that we are all seated together. As a family, we do not always take our meals together."

Devon stole a glance at Petra, who was smiling with what seemed like exaggerated innocence. Then from the corner of his eye he observed Don Felipe, who was scowling at the salt shaker. Devon thought the scene might be comical until he saw Don Felipe raise his eyes and take an appraising view of Petra, whose expression quickly turned to one of disdain. Don Felipe's eyes fell to the salt shaker again.

Consuelo came in with two bowls of soup, which she set down in front of the two ladies. She left and came back with two more for the men. With no comment, the four of them picked up their spoons and began the meal.

Devon gave his attention to the taste of

the soup, which seemed to be made from diced potatoes and bits of dried meat. He liked the taste of the black pepper.

Petra's voice came out in a cheery tone. "This is one of Consuelo's best soups. How good that she serves it when the artist is here." She directed her smile at him. "It will help you remember the best things about us."

Devon nodded, then glanced at Don Felipe, who had a sullen cast to his face as he kept his eyes lowered.

Petra turned now to her mother. "We don't know how long he will be with us, so we must treat him well when we can. A man of talent and intelligence — you were right about that, Mama, although he is always very modest."

Devon looked at his own bowl.

"Do you think we could persuade him," Petra went on, "to stay longer? He could do your portrait."

"Oh, he should do yours," said Emilia in a teasing voice.

"Only to practice. What do you think, señor *artista*? Could you do it?"

Devon cleared his throat. "It is not my best skill, as I said the other day. I have done very few portraits, and they have not come out well. Not in my opinion."

"You could practice with Petra," said the mother.

"Yes," said the daughter. "And then you could turn your real talent to a worthy topic. Don't you think my mother is beautiful, señor *artista?*"

"Well, of course." Devon could feel Don Felipe's glare as, in response to Petra's question, he looked across the table to give Emilia a most perfunctory smile. His glance fell on the silver cross that lay on her blouse, and the sight of it put him at ease.

"Then how can you resist?" Petra continued. "You can do mine first, as she suggests. I will sit motionless for days." She held her head up with her lips in a pout. "You will say it is terrible, and I will say fine. We will tear it up, burn it. Then you will do one of my mother. You will say you cannot. We will insist. Then you will give in, and you will find it easy. Simple. The beauty, the grace, the perfection will inspire you."

"You are very cheerful," said Devon. "I am sure you do not make light of me, for it is all in praise of your mother, but I am also sure I could not do it."

"Can't you see," came the stern voice of Don Felipe, "that he doesn't want to?"

Petra, still in her airy voice, responded, "Oh, but I hope to convince him."

196

"He says the same thing he said the other day."

"Yes, but that was when you said you would not be a worthy subject. You must agree that such could not be the case with my mother. She is most worthy, and she would bring out the best of the artist's talent."

Don Felipe gave a nod of recognition toward his wife. "Of course she is most worthy. But it would be very discourteous to make the artist feel as if it were an obligation."

Petra smiled again at Devon. "It is his modesty only. Is it not?"

"I do believe," he answered, "in all honesty, that I lack the talent."

"As I said, pure modesty. But set the beautiful woman before you, with no distractions, and the result would be a marvel."

Devon smiled again at Emilia, this time with less restraint. "All that your daughter says is true, except that I would have the talent. I beg you to believe me that I would be very clumsy, and it would embarrass me, in spite of the excellent model."

"Do not fear," said the gracious lady. "Nobody is going to ask you to do something that would make you feel uncomfortable."

Devon nodded in appreciation.

"I'm not done yet," said Petra, still in her laughing tone. "But we'll let this topic go for the time being."

Consuelo took away the soup bowls two at a time and on the return trip replaced them with plates of chicken and rice. As Devon set about using his knife and fork to separate the thigh meat from its bone, Petra's voice came up again."

"Please tell us, señor *artista,* do you hunt birds where you live?"

Devon paused to think of the right words for his answer. "I have hunted ducks, and a small bird, smaller than a pigeon or a dove. About this size." He held up his closed fist.

"Codorniz," said Don Felipe.

"Is that what it is?" asked Petra.

"A small bird," Devon went on. "It runs on the ground, and it flies."

"Codorniz," repeated the master, this time raising his head and giving a hard stare.

"How do you call it in English?" Petra asked.

"It is called *quail.*"

"And how do you hunt them?" she continued.

"With a shotgun," Don Felipe answered.

"Yes, with a shotgun."

"Ducks and quail both?" asked Emilia.

"Yes. The little pellets disperse." Devon sprayed out his fingers to illustrate the idea.

"I've eaten duck," said Emilia. "It is very good."

"Oh, I would love to have duck again," Petra put in. "Perhaps you could bring me some. Do you shoot many?"

"It is very far."

She smiled. "Oh, yes. And how do you cook the quail?"

"In a sauce, usually. One needs several to make a meal."

"Like the *tórtola*," said Don Felipe.

Devon looked up, and Emilia must have caught his uncertain look, for she said, "The gray dove."

He nodded.

"How interesting," Petra continued. "Is it true that some men hunt only for sport, that they do not eat what they hunt?"

"I believe so. They give it away."

"To the servants."

Devon shrugged. "To them, or to friends, or to the poor people."

"Ah, yes." After a pause she added, "So are you good with the shotgun?"

"Normal. I don't go out very much."

She narrowed her eyes. "I'm sure you are very good, and you are being modest again. Don't you think so, Mama?"

"Maybe."

After the chicken and rice, Consuelo brought out a flan, or custard. Don Felipe finished his in no time and lit a cigarette, while Devon, following the example of the women, carved off a little at a time with his spoon.

"I am very interested in your customs," Petra began. "Do you go to the theater?"

"At times. Especially if I am in a larger city."

"Oh, I just love the theater. And the opera? Do you go to hear it?"

"Not so much. More the theater."

"And museums?"

"I go to see art exhibits, and sometimes historical ones."

"Historical?"

"Yes, artifacts from earlier times. Some exhibits travel. For example, there was one of the Spanish. Uniforms, helmets, swords, that sort of thing. And another of findings from Egypt."

"I was in a museum once. My father took me when we were in the Republic. It was a museum that was dedicated to birds. All birds. Many beautiful ones — tropical parrots and other curious things, in very pretty colors. Some of them were two, three, four, all the same."

"There are museums of that kind, also. Natural history. Even unto fishes and snakes." He glanced at Don Felipe, who registered no response behind his cloud of smoke.

"And when you go, do you go alone?"

"Sometimes."

"You go with girls, don't you? With ladies. Oh, I'm sorry. That is an indiscreet question."

"No, that's all right. I'm not that delicate."

She narrowed her eyes again as she paused with a dab of custard on the tip of her spoon. "I imagine you have many girls who go after you."

He laughed. "No, not really."

"Oh, yes," she teased. "You are being modest again. You don't want to say. But you, with your blond hair and blue eyes, I'm sure there are many who look for you."

Devon did not consider his sandy hair to be blond, but he did not think it was anything to contradict. "I don't know."

"Don't you think so, Mama? With blond hair and blue eyes, all the girls look for him?"

"Maybe."

"They don't insist very much," he said.

"You didn't leave any sad ones waiting for you?"

"I don't think so."

"And you're not running from any?" She gave him a playful look.

"Not that I know of."

"Then maybe you did not come here just to look at old churches."

"I came here to see all the wonders of landscapes, vistas, and sad old ruins."

"And to paint only those things." She put her lips into a pout again.

"I see we're back to that topic."

"Perhaps we are. I thought perhaps you did not want to do a portrait of a lady because you were afraid someone would be jealous."

"Oh, no. Even if there were someone, my art is my own."

Petra laid her pretty hand on the table between them. "That is good. I may convince you yet — you of the pretty blue eyes — to do a portrait of a subject worthy of your art."

Don Felipe's voice came up. "The artist has already stated that he does not wish to do portraits. For his own reasons, he prefers to do rundown buildings and cracked walls." Don Felipe's tense eyes accentuated his prominent cheekbones as he drew in on the cigarette and then expelled the smoke.

Petra turned to her mother. "The artist

has said he is afraid to try, but I do not believe it. I think that, in truth, he is brave, just as he is handsome. What do you think, Mama?"

Emilia gave Devon a kind smile. "Maybe."

Don Felipe finished his second cigarette and stood up, reaching for his sombrero. "I am going to work," he said.

Emilia looked up at him. "With *el tordillo?*"

"Yes." Then to all three at the table he said, *"Con permiso,"* and left with his spurs clinking.

Devon caught Emilia's attention. "What was that word you used?"

"¿El tordillo?"

"Yes."

"It means gray. A gray horse."

"Oh, I understand. Thank you." He looked at both ladies. "Well, it has been a great pleasure. Thank you very much for the meal. I believe that I, too, must go back to my work."

"Do not forget," said Petra.

Devon pointed to his head. "Always present." He rose from his chair.

"I'll go out with you," said Petra, tossing her napkin on the table and pushing back her chair.

"Thank you for coming." Emilia rose from her chair and walked to the end of the table, where she gave Devon her hand. "Remember that you are always welcome here."

"Thank you," he said, meeting her soft brown eyes. "You are very generous."

As Devon and Petra walked into the living room, Consuelo appeared with his hat.

"Thank you."

"Que le vaya bien." May all go well for you.

Once outside in the *portal,* Petra had less of her bright and sparkling demeanor. "Have a good afternoon," she said. "I hope you progress in your work."

"Thank you. I hope you and your mother have a restful afternoon. It was a very enjoyable dinner."

"I'm glad you enjoyed it."

Devon lingered. "Do you have a routine in the afternoon? Do you read? I think you said the other day that you do."

"Sometimes. Today I'm going to read in my catechism."

"Oh, that's good."

"And my mother plans to go to give consolation to Ricardo's family."

"Does she go alone?"

"No, Consuelo goes with her. And Miguel, of course."

"That's good. I hope she has a safe trip."

"Thank you." She gave him her hand, bare and pretty as he had seen it last. "Until next time, señor *artista*."

"Until then, señorita Cantera."

He walked out into the bright sunlight, where Don Felipe was leading the gray horse to the snubbing post.

El tordillo. La tórtola. El codorniz. His words for the day.

The master did not give him so much as a glance as he untied the horse, let him drink, and walked him out a few paces before tightening the cinch. Then Devon swung aboard, and with the master at his back, he rode out past the dark pool and the cottonwood trees and through the stone gateway of Rancho Agua Prieta, onto the open plain.

CHAPTER TEN

With a glass of beer in front of him, Devon felt at home in the dim interior of La Sombra. The items on the wall — the thick spurs, the coiled bullwhip, the stretched rattlesnake skin — were now as familiar as the decor of any place he frequented back home. Lalo the bartender ignored him as usual and stood at the end of the bar with a cluster of regular patrons. The large, round-shouldered man held forth in his accustomed manner, patting the others on the shoulder and telling stories to make them laugh. His full head of hair, shot with gray, was combed back neatly all the way around, and it held in place when he threw back his head and laughed.

The music had not begun yet, and Lalo was talking loud enough that Devon could follow the joke he was telling. It was about a man who was told by a genie that he would die when his burro broke wind for the third time. After the burro whoofed twice, the man whittled a wooden plug and poked it in. Halfway up the mountain with a load of sticks, he went around back to check the plug. When he lifted the tail, the plug came out like a bullet and hit him in the forehead, fulfilling the prophecy. Lalo simulated the action by hitting the top of his fist against his own head. All the men broke into laughter.

At that moment the door opened, and Alfonso made his appearance in his trademark cream-colored hat and brown leather vest. He stood for a moment with his thumbs in his belt and his shoulders thrown back, his silver tooth shining as he surveyed the place and smiled. Then he stepped forward. After he and Lalo clapped each other on the shoulder, he came to stand at the bar between Devon and the small crowd of men. Lalo set a glass and a bottle of tequila in front of him. The foreman leaned his left elbow on the bar and turned his back partway to Devon.

The door opened again and Juanito walked in, his eyelids dark in the shadow of his brow. The stubble showed on his unshaven face, and his coarse hair hung straight and uncombed. He carried his mandolin by the neck as his feet found his customary place where he could either sit on his stool or stand to play his songs.

After a few minutes of tuning, he sang a song about a girl with a wooden heart. He followed it with one about a man fated to die in prison for killing his sweetheart and his rival. Then he sang a lively song about a man who went from town to town, from cantina to cantina, knew all the nighttime ladies and deflowered many girls. This number seemed to be a favorite of Alfonso, who stood away from the bar and faced Juanito, glass in hand, and sang along.

The smell of cooked meat and fat drew Devon's attention to the end of the bar, where he recognized the man who had been selling ribs in the street next to the plaza on Sunday. A large platter of ribs now sat on the bar. Lalo dropped some coins in the vendor's hand, and the man nodded and went out the door.

Lalo divided the stack of meat onto two other plates, three in all. Two he left at the end of the bar, and the third he set in front of Alfonso. He went back to the platter, shaved off a small pile of meat, and with his thumb and first two fingers he tucked the meat into two folded corn tortillas. At his direction, one of the men took the tacos to Juanito, who set down his instrument and accepted the food as if it were his due.

The bartender came back to stand opposite to Alfonso. Raising his head and turning his good eye to Devon, he said, *"¿Gustas?"* Do you care for some?

Devon had caught a good whiff by now, and the smell of lamb and roasted fat was appealing, but he had had mutton at the inn. "No, thanks," he said. "I just finished supper."

"Very well." Lalo gave the plate half a turn, and he and Alfonso picked the ribs. It looked like greasy work, as the bartender wiped his hands several times on his apron, and Alfonso did the same on his trousers.

In a little while, the bones were all stacked on the platter, and the singing and joking resumed. Alfonso seemed to have more of a swagger than usual, and Devon wondered if it had anything to do with the foreman's wanting to impress him.

Now Juanito was singing a song about a man who rode to Rancho Peñasco, a brave man with a rifle and pistol and horse. He had been gone for many a year, and he longed to see his dear mother. At the mouth of the canyon they challenged his entry, and when he answered with pride that he came to see the señora, they shot him six times. And ever since then, at Rancho Peñasco, his ghost haunts the canyon and rides the high cliffs.

Alfonso turned his back on this song and, with both elbows on the bar, rolled a cigarette with tobacco and a cornhusk. He lit it with a long-flamed match and then drank from his glass. With the next song, a sprightly tune about a man who met a dark-haired girl and danced every dance with her, he stood again, facing Juanito and singing the verses.

The door opened, and Carlos Hernández came in. He carried himself in his jaunty way, stopping to shake hands and exchange witticisms with the men along the bar. He gave a perfunctory handshake to Alfonso and took a place at the bar on the other side of Devon.

"Good evening," he said, offering his hand.

Devon returned the greeting and shook hands. Then he said, "I'm glad to see that you came out."

"Oh, come what may." Carlos signaled to Lalo, who put a bottle and shot glass in front of him.

"And how are things going for you today?" Devon had to raise his voice, as Alfonso was singing louder as he hoisted his glass and rocked from one foot to the other.

"How's that?"

"I said, how are things going for you?"

"Oh, all right, I guess." Carlos rolled his eyes toward Alfonso. "Let's sit over here at a table."

The two of them carried their drinks to a table about twelve feet away, where Carlos sat with his back to the main part of the cantina. He positioned his glass in front of him, poured the tequila, then set the bottle back a few inches and rotated it half a turn. After what Devon interpreted to be a civilized pause, Carlos reached for his drink.

"Salud," he said, lifting the glass.

"Salud." Devon clicked his glass against the smaller one.

For all of Carlos's repose and good cheer, his face had a worried cast to it. "And for you, things went well today?"

"I suppose so."

"You went to the rancho?"

"Yes, I did, and this time I had dinner with the whole family."

"Is that so?"

"Yes, it was a little strange to see your cousin at the table with her stepfather, and on top of that, she was all cheerful."

Carlos held his eyes wide open. "And Don Felipe?"

"Serious, somewhat gruff."

"And my aunt?"

"She seemed to be happy that everyone was at the table together. As always, a very gracious lady."

"Oh, yes." Carlos touched his glass and then drew his hand back and let it rest on the table. "And what is your impression?"

"Of what?"

"Well, of the whole thing but of Don Felipe in particular."

"To tell the truth, I think your cousin was being so light and gay in order to make him uncomfortable."

"Jealous?"

"Maybe that, and maybe something else, I'm not sure. But I don't think she wanted him to enjoy the meal, and I think she realized her objective."

Carlos laughed. "She has a lot of spark."

"Yes, she does."

The concerned expression came back to Carlos's face, a cloud on his rough complexion. "But tell me of your impression of him."

"About the same as before. Actually, maybe a little different. I didn't feel as intimidated, which might be owing to his not having absolute authority. Oh, he had his mannerisms and pronouncements, but I didn't think he had all the control he wanted. Most definitely, I don't think he has the control to make her lie for him."

Now Carlos took a sip and ran his tongue across his lips. "Do you think he did it, then?"

"Like others, I think he is capable. But I don't see any traces of guilt, no remorse. If he did it, he must be very cold."

"It could well be. He has it in him to be a cruel man. I can tell it from the menacing things he has said to me."

"I believe it. Although I can't say whether I think he did it, I can't say that I think he didn't. Does that make sense?"

"Oh, yes."

"Well, so much for that. And yourself, how did it go for you?"

Carlos had a pained expression as he shook his head. "Not good. First, I had to answer all the same questions with the sheriff."

"Does he really suspect you?"

"I don't know, but he seems reluctant to try to get more evidence against Don Felipe."

"That's too bad. But he doesn't have that much on you, does he?"

"Only that I was out that night, which he seems to cherish."

"Well, if you didn't do it, you can conduct yourself with a clean conscience."

"Oh, sure."

"And besides, you come from a good family. It's not as if you were a *Comanchero* and this other man a saint. Even if your aunt and your cousin did not approve of you as a suitor, they could speak in your favor."

Carlos held his expressive brown eyes on Devon. "Señor, I spoke with my aunt today."

"Really? How did that happen?"

"I saw her in church. I went there on my own, to pray for all of this, and I saw her there, alone, in the empty church."

"Was Consuelo with her?"

"Well, yes, but otherwise she was alone."

"Were you able to speak with her?"

"Yes, thanks to God. At first she seemed not to want to, but when she saw how sad I was, she relented. She herself was sad."

"I understood that she was going to give her condolences to Ricardo's family."

"She said she went to their rancho, and they closed the door on her. Imagine, old friends."

"Did they think her husband did it?"

"They wouldn't say. They refused to talk to her. She felt very hurt."

"I imagine."

"For that reason, she came to the church in town, and that's how we happened to meet."

"Did she give any indication of what she thought about the death of Ricardo?"

"Only that it was very sad, for the young man and for his family."

"She didn't seem to think you did it?"

Carlos shook his head. "No, and I told her, I pledged in church, that I could never, never do such a thing."

"And what did that leave her to think?"

"I don't know."

"You didn't tell her, then, of her husband's threats to you?"

"Oh, no."

"Nor of his obsession with his stepdaughter?"

"Even less."

Devon frowned. "Have you told anyone else about his threats to you?"

Carlos shook his head. "Just you. I didn't think you would repeat it."

"I haven't, but it might help someone else to see how strongly obsessed he is."

"Maybe." Carlos produced a cigarette from his coat pocket and lit it.

Devon let out a low breath of exasperation. "Then you didn't mention it to the sheriff?"

"Well, no."

"Look. You told me, a few days ago, that he told you to stay away from her, to forget her, to have no illusions. I believe that's what you said."

"Something like that."

"And that whoever came near her would risk his life."

"That, too."

"And you haven't told anyone, not your aunt and not the sheriff?"

Carlos shrugged. "That's right."

"Well, look. If you tell the sheriff, he'll see that Don Felipe has made his threats to more than one person, and thus he might have had a very strong motivation to go out and find Ricardo — assuming Ricardo didn't come to the rancho in the first place."

Carlos winced and looked at his cigarette.

"You've got to tell someone."

"How can I? He told me not to."

"Wait a minute. He threatened you, and then he told you not to tell anyone? I suppose he backed that up with a threat on your life, too."

Carlos lowered his head in a defeated expression. "More or less."

"He did."

"Well, yes, he did."

"Listen, my friend. You can't let these kinds of threats keep the truth from being known."

"But my life is at risk."

"It is the other way, too, if by your silence you let people think you're guilty."

Carlos shook his head. "Oh, I don't like this."

Devon felt himself getting impatient. "You can't let this stepfather control everything. And besides, I don't even think he's able to."

Carlos took a long pull on his cigarette and held his head back as he let the smoke out through his nostrils, as if he were trying to build himself up.

Devon decided to give him another nudge. "The cure for this kind of thing is to get the truth out into the open."

Carlos wavered, and then his repose crumbled. "What good am I?" he said. "Who would believe me?" He dropped the cigarette on the floor and stepped on it. His face was an expression of pure misery. "And they are right. I don't deserve her."

Devon stared at him. The man was powerless. He was so unstrung by his hopeless love for his cousin and so afraid of the master of the rancho that he could not bring himself to give anything like pubic testimony. "I don't know," said Devon, "but I don't think it's right to let someone ride over the top of everyone."

■ ■ ■ ■

Devon stood at the bar by himself again. Carlos had taken his sorrow homeward, and the night had worn on a couple of hours since Devon first came in. Alfonso was still on his feet, but he had a slur to his voice and was talking loudly. Two of the other regular patrons were standing near him, also wobbling. The music had stopped for a moment, and Devon could pick out words.

"I give the orders at the rancho," Alfonso said, and the other two nodded. "The master is too busy with his horses and the other things he is trying to tame."

A laugh rippled through the two men. One of them said something that Devon didn't catch.

"She's a fine little pullet," said Alfonso, "but not worth all the trouble." He smiled, and his silver tooth glinted. "A man has to stay out of trouble. That's how he manages to be the boss." He tipped up his glass.

"And that's how you're going to be able to give us good jobs at the rancho, eh?" said the man who had spoken before.

Alfonso leered. "With what I know, I might be the master of the rancho myself before long."

The other two men laughed, and a motion just beyond them caught Devon's attention. Cayetano the moocher had finally shown up. He stuck out his chin and stretched his neck, as if he were swallowing what he just heard. Behind him stood an older, bearded man who had all the demeanor of being another hanger-on.

Time to leave, Devon told himself. As he downed the last of his beer, Juanito began another song. It was the *corrido* about the dead suitor. Alfonso was smiling, wagging his head as he rocked on his heels. Devon pushed away from the bar and headed for the door, brushing past Cayetano and the bearded man. He would have liked to hear the song again, but once he was on his way, he knew he needed to follow through. In addition, he thought it was a good bet that he would get to hear the song again before long.

Down the unlit streets he walked in the moonlight, knowing his way almost as well as Juanito on his rounds. When Devon came to the house with the solid door and no windows, he mounted the step and listened. He heard soft voices within. As his heartbeat picked up, he rapped on the door frame. The voices quieted, and he heard footsteps.

Then the door opened, and the wide-faced woman appeared with the light falling out around her.

"What is it?" she asked.

"It is I. You remember me. I've been here two other times."

Her reddish hair showed as she moved her head to let the light fall on him. "Oh, yes. Come in."

She stepped aside and let him into the parlor. Perhaps because he had heard voices, he thought he detected the warmth and scent of women in the air as he stood in their recent presence. He heard the woman click the latch on the door.

"Do you wish to see the girls?" she asked as she passed behind him.

"I do not need to see more than one, if she is available."

"Let me see." The madam stepped across the room, her high heels sounding on the floor as her hips shifted back and forth. She paused at the curtained doorway and spoke Ramona's name. After that she rattled a sentence in which Devon heard himself identified as the blond American. The buxom woman passed through the curtain, and Ramona came out.

She was wearing a seductive black dress, low-cut at the top and close-fitting at the waist. Her loose dark hair spilled down around her shoulders, and her dark eyes sparkled. From her forehead to her chest, the bronze complexion was lovely.

"A pleasure to see you again," she said. "Would you like to sit down?"

"Thank you."

She led the way to the divan and let him sit down first; then she sat next to him with her hip touching his. "And you continue to have a good stay in Tinaja?"

"Oh, yes."

"They treat you well?"

"Everyone is courteous. It would be impossible to complain."

She laid the back of her hand against his thigh. "And I hope we have treated you well here."

"Excellent." He let his gaze travel across the smooth bronze texture of her skin from the indentation of her throat to the top of her bosom. Then he lifted his eyes to meet hers, soft and dark. A field of energy hung in the air. "You are very nice," he said, "and if ever I had an ailment, you have been the best medicine."

"You speak well. Where did you learn Spanish?"

"In school, and then at work. I practice with the other workers."

"Oh, yes? What kind of work?"

"As a gardener, planting trees, then in a restaurant, and later in a warehouse."

"It serves you well in your travel, doesn't it?"

"I would like to travel more. As I said last time, I have not been to Mexico, but I would like to go."

"You will enjoy it." She touched his leg again. "And what of your visit tonight, to little Mexico?"

He felt his pulse jump, and he smiled. "Like before? The same thing? Does that suit you?"

"Oh, yes. If you like it."

"I would be enthralled."

He watched her stand up and smooth her dress, and then he followed her to the hallway, watching her shape as she walked.

In the room he gave her a silver dollar, which she laid on the dresser top with a small clack. He sat on the edge of the bed and she stood facing him, her arms raised and her hands on her head. He reached up and around her, feeling for the buttons, and released them one by one. No need to hurry. She let the dress fall to the floor, and then he held her hand as she stepped out of it, picked it up, and set it on the chair. Now he reached for the hooks and undid her corset, slipping it downward and bringing more of her beautiful bronze skin into view. Lastly he slipped off her underpants, caressing her buttocks as he pressed the side of his face against her abdomen. She put her arms around him and brought him closer, and he lost himself in the smell of her bath powder and the texture of her skin as her long dark hair fell on his cheek.

Later, as he lay under the covers with her, he dared to broach a subject. "I don't suppose you are allowed to know any of your visitors outside of this place."

"No, not here."

"It is all business."

"Here, yes."

"In Tinaja."

"Yes."

"What if I ever saw you somewhere else?"

"For example?"

"If I ever went to the Republic."

"Oh, I don't know how you would find me."

"You don't have an address there?"

"No, not now."

He sensed that if he went any further he would cross a line into an area outside the bounds of the present arrangement. "It is difficult, then."

"Perhaps."

"Well, even if it is just business, it is very enchanting."

"Thank you. You are very nice. And gentle." She sat up on the edge of the bed and reached for her clothes.

He did the same on his side. After a few minutes she came around to let him button her up. She stood with her back to him, and he passed his hands over her hips before reaching for the buttons on her dress.

"Is this your last visit, then? Are you leaving?"

"I hope not. I haven't planned when I'm going to leave, but I think I'll manage to come here once again, if only to say goodbye."

She turned around and straightened her dress. "That would be fine."

He stood up and finished buttoning his shirt. "When I come back I can give you my address, already written on a piece of paper. Then if you ever wanted, if you were in another place, you could write me."

She put her hand on his cheek. "You don't know me."

He smiled. "That's true. But I'll come by here, one way or the other, before I leave town. Is that all right?"

"I will always be happy to see you."

"Perfect." He reached into his pocket and took out another silver dollar. "This is for you, not to share with the señora. If you want to buy something nice for yourself and remember me for it, that's fine, and if you want to put it in your savings to start your business, that's up to you."

"Thank you." She crossed the room, opened a dresser drawer, and deposited the coin without a sound.

At that distance, he could see her as a woman who had accommodated other men, and he had a fleeting thought, once again wondering whether the late Ricardo Vega had ever known pleasures such as these. When she turned, he sensed that their intimacy was ended for this time.

He sat on the edge of the bed again and leaned over to pull on his boots. "It's too bad about the young man who died," he said.

"Oh, yes. We heard of that. Poor boy." She stepped into her shoes.

"My friend Carlos is troubled about it, too."

"Carlos has a good heart."

"Yes, and he is afraid some people will think he did it."

She leaned her head back and shook her hair, then straightened the front of her dress again. "Oh, I think what most people say is probably the truth, that it is just a matter of whether anyone wants to do anything about it." She held out her hand to help him stand up. "Very well, señor *artista.* Everything fine?"

"Everything's perfect. I feel brand-new."

CHAPTER ELEVEN

At breakfast, Devon's most pleasant thought was of his visit to little Mexico, as Ramona had phrased it. He recalled how she touched his leg when she said it, and the memory brought a smile to his face. Her preference to keep things on a business basis left a lingering bittersweet effect, but it hadn't diminished the pleasure, and it was probably good judgment. Who wanted good judgment, though, when he was close to a presence like hers?

His thoughts wandered to less enchanting topics, such as the predicament of Carlos. Paralyzed and helpless, he would seem pathetic if it weren't for his congeniality and if he didn't remind Devon of his own passivity, which he hoped he was shedding.

Interwoven with his impressions of Carlos were some less sympathetic ones of Don Felipe. To Devon it seemed evident that the master of the rancho had either killed

Ricardo or had him killed, and in addition to having no remorse, he seemed to be successful at keeping others from saying or doing anything. And there was still a puzzle there. Devon did not think Don Felipe had the power to coerce Petra to lie for him, for she clearly loathed him and showed no sign of being under his will, but it still seemed as if she hadn't told the whole truth when she answered the sheriff's questions.

Regardless of whether she varied the story, however, there were still two wrongs that were not being set right. One was that someone, probably Don Felipe, was not being made to answer for Ricardo's death; the other was that Don Felipe could get away with making Carlos keep his mouth shut. The basic injustice and Carlos's compliance grated on Devon to the point that he decided it was unacceptable to let things go along on their own. Somebody had to do something, and it was clear that it wasn't going to be Carlos. On a more subtle level, it looked as if it wasn't going to be Petra, even though she had knowledge of Don Felipe's obsession and was not afraid to act.

When he had finished his breakfast of fried potatoes, bacon, and eggs, he handed in his room key and went out to stand on the front step of the inn. He felt as if his body was taking the sun's energy right in; it made him feel strong and capable.

He looked up and down the street. A man in drab clothes and a straw hat was watering a burro in the stone trough. The animal was carrying a load of sticks, which reminded Devon of the joke he had heard the night before. It also made him wonder how far away the man had to go to find even slender firewood such as that.

Devon stepped onto the sidewalk and turned. Down the street in the other direction, across from the town square and in the middle of the block, sat the sheriff's office. Devon had walked past it a few times on his way to and from the place where he visited Ramona. His footsteps led him there now, without his having formally acknowledged to himself that he was going to speak with the tall-hatted, mustachioed Bonifacio. But that was the image he had in his mind now, and he knew that was where he was going.

He rapped twice without getting an answer, so he tried the handle and pushed the door open. As he looked around the empty office, a heavy wood door opened in the back. A slender man with his head lowered was standing a step lower in a hallway that apparently led to the jail area. With both hands he lifted on the rope handle of a wooden mop bucket, complete with mop sticking out, and swung it up onto the office floor. As he straightened up, Devon recognized him as the bearded man he had seen with Cayetano the night before.

"How can I help you, sir?" The man stepped into the room.

"Is the sheriff here?"

"Not right now, but he won't be long."

"A few minutes? An hour?"

"Not long. Have a seat if you please."

During the exchange, the man gave no indication of having seen Devon before, although Devon was sure that as the blond American he was conspicuous enough to be remembered. He took a seat in one of the two empty oak chairs across from the sheriff's desk as the janitor stepped back down into the hallway and closed the door behind him.

A minute later the door opened again, and the sheriff appeared. With his hand on his knee he pushed himself up into the room. Once there, he stood up straight and pulled on his waistband. He was dressed very much as he had been before, with a dark brown hat, a plain brown vest, and a gray shirt. He was not wearing his pistol or a belt, and his trousers came up to the underside of his belly.

"Yes, sir?"

Devon stood up, took off his hat, and made ready to shake hands. "I would like to be able to speak with you for a moment, if you please."

"That's all right. Sit down." The sheriff waved at him, crossed the room, and sat behind his desk.

Devon sat with his hat in his hand, waiting.

"Very well. Go ahead."

"Perhaps you remember me. I was present with the señorita Cantera the other day when you visited Rancho Agua Prieta."

"Of course. You are the painter."

"That's right. Well, as you know, I have become acquainted with some of the people there, as well as here in town."

The sheriff pulled at the corner of his mustache. "That's normal."

"Yes. And so I share their sentiments about the death of the young man Ricardo Vega."

"Which sentiments, precisely?"

"That it was lamentable that he died, a very bad thing, and it would only be right if his family were able to find out the truth."

"You must know the family very well, for you have learned more about their sentiments than I have."

"I have not spoken directly with Doña Emilia about the case, but I know she feels that way, and I also know that her nephew Carlos has compatible feelings."

"I would not have thought of those two first, nor would I combine them into a majority opinion."

"Be that as it may, I share the sentiment that it would be desirable to find out the truth."

The sheriff cocked his head. "I hope you do not think the idea is a novelty here."

"No. I would just like to offer my impression."

"Your impression of how desirable the truth is, or of the truth itself?"

"Well, to put it in such few words, the truth itself."

"Ah. Were you there?"

"No. By no means. But my impression is this: the master of the rancho has had the habit of threatening any young man who has expressed interest in his stepdaughter. He also threatens harm if the young man should say anything. The stepfather has a dangerous obsession, which may not be obvious in the public eye."

"What else?"

Devon felt as if he had more to say, that

he was being made to say it too quickly, and he wasn't sure how to back up and develop it better. "Well, I think his motivation deserves to be considered."

The sheriff closed his eyes and dipped his head in agreement. Then looking vaguely in Devon's direction, he said, "I have given it consideration."

"With respect, I do not wish to suggest how to do things, but I believe it could be looked into more deeply."

The sheriff frowned. "A second trp to the rancho would give me the same answers as before. Do you think either Don Felipe or the señorita would tell me anything different?"

"I don't know."

"What is needed is something new. New evidence." The sheriff folded his hands across the crown of his stomach. "You have an impression, and perhaps it is valid, but it is not enough for me to intensify my suspicion."

Devon took a few seconds to let the statement sink in. The sheriff didn't want to budge. "I wish I could make it clearer," he said.

The sheriff shook his head, and the tall hat wagged back and forth. "No, I understand you. You speak well."

Devon stood up. "Thank you all the same. I appreciate that you listen to me."

"At your service."

Devon walked out into the sunlight and put on his hat. Ten minutes earlier, he had the idea that the probability of Don Felipe being the culprit was an open secret. Now he wondered if, as Ramona had suggested, the sheriff was reluctant to pursue that suspicion or if he was simply waiting for new evidence. Devon looked at the sun. It could be a long wait.

He went back to the hotel and got his things together for another day of work at the old church. When he went downstairs to hand in the room key, he waited a few minutes for the innkeeper to bring him a packed lunch. The tall, dark-featured man returned to the reception area with the small bundle wrapped as usual in coarse brown paper.

"So you go again to the rancho?" he asked.

"Yes. To the old bare walls. To study."

"Oh, yes," said the innkeeper, as if he had needed a prompt to memory. After a few seconds he added, "Is that not difficult?"

"In what way?"

"Just from what one hears. That there has been danger there."

"At the church?"

"Not exactly. At the rancho."

"You refer to the unfortunate thing that happened, perhaps on that rancho but perhaps on the rancho of the young man's family."

"Yes."

"Well, I don't feel that very much danger might be directed at me. For one thing, I am not a *pretendiente* of the young lady."

"Oh, I was not speaking of that danger, although the possibility exists there as well. What I was referring to is that the young man's family is impatient for someone to do something, and they may decide, in the old way, to take care of things themselves."

Devon, sensing the need to speak on a general, discreet level, said, "The person who should do something does not seem very disposed. He says he needs more proof, but I wonder if he is trying not to get on the bad side of the master."

"It's difficult to say."

"I appreciate your mentioning it, though."

"A precaution."

"Thank you."

"You're welcome." The innkeeper made a small bow with his head. "At your service."

As Devon rode out of town toward the rancho, his hat brim blocked the glare of the sun, which was higher in the sky than it had been on recent mornings when he went to the ruins. In the warm air, the dust rose quicker and hung longer. Devon touched the horse with his heel so as not to lag.

Coming to the crest of a long, slow rise, he saw a wagon on the road about half a mile ahead. It was loaded with burlap bags of something, probably grain. He kept the horse at a good fast walk, and in a little while he came up behind the wagon, veered to the right, and passed alongside at a distance of about ten yards. Sitting straight up in the saddle, he was able to count the sacks. Twenty even — probably a month's supply of oats for the horses in the stalls. Life with its commerce and routines went on as usual.

The driver, who looked like one of the men who had lingered around the gate at the rancho, looked over his shoulder and nodded. Devon waved and rode ahead.

He took a fork to the right, a less-worn path than the road he had been on. Again he could see mountains in the distance while rises in the ground cut off objects a quarter- or half-mile away. So it was that when he looked off to the side for a moment and then brought his gaze back to the trail, he saw a rider on a brown horse ahead at the crest of a slope. The posture, the hat, and the vest were all familiar, and as Devon drew closer, he could make out the grinning effigy of a saddle horn.

He rode straight ahead on the trail, and when he came within fifty yards he saw that Alfonso was wearing a pistol and had tucked his gloves into the gunbelt. With the reins held in the crook of his left little finger, he was rolling a cigarette with tobacco grains and a cornhusk.

Devon edged off the trail and drew up about five yards away from the foreman. *"Buenos días,"* he said.

Alfonso returned the greeting, knocking the edges off the *b* and the *d.*

"I'm on my way to the old church. I hope there's not a problem"

The foreman pushed his lips out and shook his head. Then he popped a match, lit his cigarette, shook out the match, and held it. "Not at all. The master just likes to know who is on his land and for what purpose."

Devon inferred that he was to give an account of himself. "I just came from town. I passed a wagon that had twenty sacks of grain, it looked like, and I turned to come this way."

Alfonso shrugged, as if it wouldn't have occurred to him to ask a personal question.

"And I've seen nothing out of the ordinary except a dead snake."

An eyebrow lifted. "That's normal, too. If one knows the country, he sees a great many snakes, dead and alive."

"I'm always careful around them."

"That's the best." Alfonso dropped the dead match on the ground.

Devon touched the brim of his hat. "Very well. I'll be on my way. Until later."

Alfonso shifted in the saddle and blew out a cloud of smoke. "Until later."

Left to himself at the church ruins, Devon sifted his thoughts. Public opinion seemed to have settled into a common idea, but to no real effect, and even if Don Felipe was making a good show of being nonchalant and stonewalling any suspicions, he had not brought everything under his control. There was a chink somewhere, or he wouldn't have his foreman out spying.

Devon poked around, going from one scene in the ruins to another without finding anything to absorb his attention for more than a halfhearted sketch. Time and again he drifted to the window opening where Petra habitually appeared, but all he saw was the dry plains. Although he couldn't define why, he felt that she was the key to the problem, and he wished he could have another chance to talk to her.

He didn't think it would do to ride straight to the house and ask for her. When he was invited, he felt justified, but it would be too forward and ill-advised to go there on his own. He recalled Don Felipe's warning not to seek other things, and although he interpreted it to mean romantic interest, it gave boundaries all the same. On the other hand, Doña Emilia and Petra had given him to understand that he was always welcome to drop by on a social visit, and he felt that he could take their word on that.

Devon gave another thought to Alfonso's vigilance. The foreman seemed to be on the lookout to see who was going where, not to block the artist from going to the rancho itself. Still, if he and his horrid saddle decoration were to show up on the road as Don Felipe had done a couple of days earlier, Devon would find it discouraging.

He went back to looking at dull walls of adobe, and when the sun was straight up and cast the thinnest shadows of the day, he took out his cold tortillas with meat and ate his lunch.

When the shadows had crept out a couple of feet, he happened to be standing at the window again, looking out, when he saw a lone rider crossing the plain and heading southwest. It was Don Felipe, a black figure on a white horse, with the wide sombrero visible over a half-mile away. The horse was traveling at an easy lope, raising a small cloud of dust as it went. After a long minute it disappeared behind the corner of the building. Devon walked through the church to the other side, where he waited at a window opening. Within a few minutes the horse and rider came into view again, still angling southwest.

Now would be the time to visit, if he was willing to take the chance of crossing paths with Alfonso. Devon hemmed and hawed, tried to go back to his work, and finally packed up his pencils and pads and set off.

He found the road clear on the way to the rancho, and the gatekeeper, who was not the same man who had been driving the wagon, opened the gate for him. As Devon rode through the stone entrance, he thought the place had an empty feel to it. Maybe it was just because he knew the master had gone away. The pool sat quiet on his left, and the horses in the stalls on his right made little noise. He did not see the wagon or the sacks of grain, which did not surprise him. That little piece of work would have been absorbed into the earlier part of the day.

His horse stopped at the stone water trough, so he swung down and let it drink. Then he tied it at the hitching rail and went to knock at the *portal.*

The walk-through door was ajar, and he could hear raised voices from within. From the sounds of it, mother and daughter were having an argument. At first the voices were indistinct, and then he heard Petra, loud and clear.

"It's all your fault for having married him in the first place. That, and tolerating his overbearing manner!"

Devon rapped as hard as he could with his penknife on the wood frame, two series of loud knocks.

The voices quieted. He heard footsteps, then the house door opening. Consuelo appeared in the doorway. Worry showed on her creased face, but she wiped her hands on her apron and assumed a calm demeanor.

"Yes, sir?"

"Excuse me. Pardon me for interrupting, but I was passing by and decided to stop in and say hello. Perhaps it is not a good time."

"Just a minute. Let me see."

Devon stood in silence with the sun

warming his back and glancing off the painted lumber.

Consuelo reappeared. "Come in, please. The ladies are at home."

Devon took off his hat and followed her into the house, where Doña Emilia came forward to meet him. She was wearing a dark gray dress, with the silver cross shining as she moved, and she had a distraught expression on her face.

"Oh, good afternoon, señor *artista*. It is good to see you. My daughter and I were having a few cross words, which it gives me pain for you to hear. But you know, we are just people, with our defects. Now that you are here, it will be good to have a change in subject. Come in and sit down." She gave him her hand to touch and then led the way to the sitting area.

Petra, in a dark red dress and with her hair tied back as always, gave him her hand as well. Her face looked clouded, as if her anger had not subsided, and she gave a smile that seemed to admit as much. "Put yourself at ease," she said. "We are just arguing like women."

When the three of them had taken seats, Devon and Petra each on a couch and Emilia in a leather-padded chair with Consuelo behind her, the mother spoke first.

"And how goes your work today?"

"So-so, I'd say. Some days are better than others. Everything that presented itself today was slow and dull. Very little inspiration."

"And so you came by here, to improve the day?" said Petra, with a nervous laugh.

Devon put on a gallant expression. "Yes, to add some sweetness to a day that had lost its flavor."

"Isn't it true?" said Emilia. "As if the atmosphere were bad."

"Do you find it so?" added Petra. "Perhaps the atmospheric conditions are too heavy, and they weigh on the spirit."

"Perhaps. I sense it in town as well."

Petra glanced at her mother and then at him. "Is that right? And what do you think it is owing to?"

Devon hesitated, but having taken the first step already, he pushed on. "I think it is the matter that brought the sheriff here the other day. Not a comfortable topic, perhaps."

Emilia shook her head. "It is very sad. Ricardo's family is full of bitterness, and not without reason."

"So it seems," Devon offered. "For their loss, of course, and then the sheriff seems unwilling to do anything."

"They didn't tell me that much." She looked at her hands, which she held folded in her lap, and then she raised her eyes to meet his. "Tell me what they say in town."

"Well," he began, "as you know, the people always say many things. But it is well known, as the sheriff said the other day, that Don Felipe, with your permission, made threats to the young man Ricardo."

"Yes, that is known." She had a grimace on her face as if in admission of shame, but she did not say more.

"And on the basis of that, people believe that Ricardo may have met his death here."

"At Rancho Agua Prieta?"

Devon closed his eyes and opened them as he made a small nod. "Yes. And furthermore, your nephew Carlos, whom I have come to know, has told me more than once that Don Felipe made similar threats to him."

Emilia's face tensed. "This I did not know."

"Carlos has not spoken of it in public."

"Ah, Carlos. He does not want to offend anyone."

"He is cautious, especially in this case." Devon paused. "He believes Don Felipe is dangerous."

"I don't know how much." Her soft brown

eyes did not waver, and her face held steady.

"Nor do I," said Devon, glancing at Petra, who was keeping silent. "But it seems as if his intimidation of young men, some of which I have seen directed towards me, arises from his jealousy."

Doña Emilia shook her head as before. "It could be. I myself have had that thought, and now my husband has gone away."

Devon recalled the lone rider crossing the plain, and he wondered how to connect the two parts of Emilia's statement. "I am sorry if you have had trouble," he said.

"Well, it cannot change my love for him, and for that my daughter still blames me."

Petra straightened up and sat forward in her seat, and her eyes blazed. In her red dress, she seemed like a fire that had exploded. "I don't see how you can love him! Not when I have told you, as I just have, of all the times he has come close to me and touched me and tried to convince me to be his."

Emilia's eyes shifted from Petra to Devon and back to Petra, and Devon felt his own eyes widen.

The fire flared again. "Because of his sick love, he has tried to keep all others away, thinking he can have me for himself. And now that he knows you know, he has gone away." Petra held her chin up, with an expression of thorough contempt on her face.

She's got nerve, Devon thought. *She's saying it this way to make it public.*

Emilia glanced up and around, with the same haunted look that Devon had seen on an earlier visit. "How can you say these things in front of a stranger, someone from outside the family?" Then she burst into tears, covered her face with her hands, and got up. *"Con permiso,"* she said, then hurried from the room with Consuelo behind her.

Devon turned to let his eyes meet Petra's.

She was solid as a rock, with a calm, combative air about her. "It is true. The master of the rancho with his dirty hands. But I don't think it is a great surprise to you, from what you say."

"Not really. But it is different to hear it out loud, in front of his wife."

Petra raised her eyebrows. "She has let herself remain blind to the whole affair. It's time someone took the bandage from her eyes."

"It takes courage, I can say that." He tipped her a nod of recognition. "But it gives her great pain." He looked in the direction where Emilia had gone. "Just as it does to hear us talking about it now, even if she can't hear the words."

"Well, then, we can go outside. We won't bother anyone there, and no one will bother us." She rose from her seat and stood at attention.

Devon stood with his hat in his hand. "Go ahead."

Chapter Twelve

Devon and Petra walked out of the *portal* into the bright afternoon. The sun was starting to slip in the west, hanging a little above eye level at the moment, but its rays felt strong in this area where the heat had collected all day.

"Let's go to the trees," she said, "for the shade."

They crossed the hard, bare middle area of the parade ground. Devon's hat protected him from the strength of the sun, but Petra had not brought her parasol or any other form of shade, so her white complexion and red dress were shining. In a few minutes the glare was cut by the cool shadows of the cottonwood trees.

It was the closest Devon had come to the dark pool. He noted the rocks that lined the edge, absorbed by the earth and lined with moss along the surface of the water. He could not see very far down into the pool, so he had no idea how deep it was or what lay along its bottom. From the first time he saw it he had assumed it was artesian.

"This is a nice spot," he said.

"I don't come here very much because of the dust and dirt. And when I was a little girl, I was always told to stay away. My mother was afraid I would fall in, and my father did not like me out here where the men were, anyway."

Devon raised his chin and peered out to the center of the surface. "A good precaution." Then, noting again the stones around the edge, he asked, "Does anyone use this as a source of water?"

"The rabbits come to drink," she said, "and every once in a while, a deer. At one time, long ago, the livestock drank here, but they broke down the sides and made a big mess, and some of them fell in and drowned. That's what my father told me. Therefore someone, in the time of his father or grandfather, lined the edge and planted these trees. Since then, the animals drink in their own places." She waved her hand at the rest of the compound.

"The wells must not be very deep here. I have seen two hand-pumps outside here, and I suppose you have one in the kitchen."

"The water is very accessible."

"That would be why they put the house and corrals here to begin with. Does the rancho take its name from this pool?"

"Yes. Rancho Agua Prieta, for the dark water. My father was very proud of having good water, of course." She began to walk, taking slow, wandering steps.

He walked beside her, watching the ground ahead. "I'm sure." Silence hung in the air for a minute until he spoke again. "And this other one?"

"He does not like dogs or chickens or peacocks or even sheep, although they bring him money. He likes only his precious horses."

"And so he has gone away. Just in a pout, or did he really leave?"

"I don't know. I can't believe he would leave that easily. If I know him, he probably went to tie up some bank accounts so he can keep his leverage."

"Depending on how much public opinion matters to him, he may not enjoy the reception he receives."

"Pah!" she said. "He deserves to be despised for much more than what is circulating in the current gossip, though that is plenty in itself."

Devon kept his eyes on her as he asked his question. "Do you think he was the cause of Ricardo's death?"

Still ambling along, she arched an eyebrow and looked sideways at him. "I know he was."

He stopped. "You know it?"

She stopped as well, and turning, she brought her dark eyes to meet his. "I saw him."

Just for a moment his surroundings seemed to swim and blur. Then he got command of his senses. "You saw him? On the night in question?"

"Yes." She paused, but she did not seem reluctant to tell more. "It was Saturday. Ricardo sent word that he would come at night, around midnight. He said he would come by the orchard, and he would whistle."

"So you waited up, as you told the sheriff."

"Yes. And I knew Don Felipe was still up as well. I heard him moving around, and I smelled his cigarette smoke. I knew also that he had a horse saddled and ready. Consuelo told me, as she heard it from Miguel."

"And so Ricardo came?"

"As he said. At a little after midnight. I heard a long, low whistle. I went to the window and opened it. The moon was up, lighting the night."

"Just a couple of days before the full moon."

"It was bright, but I couldn't see him. Then I heard Don Felipe leave the house, so I followed him. He went out through the *portal,* went to the stable, and brought out a white horse. He climbed on and went out the gate, slow at first."

"Did he have someone at the gate?"

"Yes. You could see it was all planned."

"Did you follow him?"

"No. I went out the other way, through the orchard, listening for Ricardo. But he didn't whistle again. Then I heard the hooves of a horse, loud and hard, as Don Felipe came around the outside." She pointed in the direction of the horse stalls. "I went to the edge of the trees, and I saw Ricardo on his horse, maybe a hundred yards away, out on the plain. Don Felipe yelled at him to stop, called him a coward. So he waited."

"Had he already started to leave?"

"I don't believe so. I think he was uncertain and had withdrawn a ways, planning to come back. I don't know for sure, of course."

"And so Don Felipe caught up with him?"

"Oh, yes, in a great fury. He knocked him off his horse, rode circles around him, and shot him four times. Then he left him there on the ground."

Devon raised his eyebrows and shook his head. "So much for his word and his honor. Based on what he told the sheriff, he would proudly take responsibility if he carried out his threat, but it is evident that once he did it, he didn't want to face the consequences if he could get away with it."

"Exactly," she said, with the look of contempt again on her face. "He left Ricardo there, sent Alfonso out to transport the body, and then instructed all the workers to say that they heard and knew nothing."

"And your mother?"

"If she heard anything from inside the house, I don't know, but if she did, she might prefer not to know what it was."

Devon let out a long breath. "It is all very clear," he said, "except one thing. Why did you lie to the sheriff and protect him?"

Her eyes were like two polished pieces of coal. "I did it to punish him for all the times he tried to impose himself on me."

"To punish him?"

"Yes. To make him twist in pain, knowing that at any moment I chose, I could turn him in."

Devon knew the word for blackmail, but he chose not to use it. "For control," he said.

"Precisely. And then, shameless and brazen as he is, he went so far as to tell me I lied to protect him."

"It would seem that way."

"*Pah!* Trash that he is, dirt and filth, he told me I lied to protect him because I knew I was going to be his."

"When did he tell you this?"

"Last night, in his repugnant manner. And for that reason, today I divulged his motives to my mother. I had suggested it to her many times before, and this time I told her, in pointed words and in front of him, that he tried to take advantage of me. Yet she insists on sticking by this . . . abuser . . . come what may."

"So that was the occasion for the big dispute, earlier in the day."

"Yes."

"Did he ride away in shame, then?"

"Him? He does not have enough shame. I think he saw it as a momentary defeat, and since he didn't have things under control in his own way, he went to regroup his forces."

Devon thought back to his earlier impression that she had staged the disclosure with him in front of her mother in order to give it an audience. That was strengthening her control. "We have a saying in English," he said. "When someone makes a personal disgrace public, we call it hanging out the dirty laundry."

"We have a similar saying, to bring out all the rags."

"Yes, and you know, if there has been a sickness in the house, with deadly germs, it is a good practice to take out all the blankets and sheets and mattresses, and expose them to the sun for a day or two."

"Oh, yes. To kill the germs."

"Well, I think you have a good impulse in wanting to expose this man for his attempts on you. Perhaps if he had succeeded, as happens in some cases, a sense of shame would discourage you, but you are in a good position to use the truth."

She took on a defiant, almost haughty, expression. "Not only did he never have success, but he never received the least interest or encouragement."

"Nor would I have thought he had. What I am focusing on is the possibility of killing germs by exposing them to sunlight."

She seemed to settle down somewhat as she said, "Very well."

He chose his words with care. "It is good that you can speak of these things with me — that is, with another person."

"You are a person of confidence and intelligence."

"I appreciate that, but perhaps I should

not be the only one. Do you think, perhaps, that you would be willing to tell others what you know?"

"Others? In what way?"

"I think your word would be more effective than mine. You could be of service if you let the truth be known, just as you have with me."

She gave him a narrow look. "Do you mean all the times when he came too close to me? Once my mother knows, and once she knows that someone else does, why does it have to go further?"

"I was not thinking so much of that. What I mean is, can you tell what you saw that night when Ricardo came here to the rancho?"

"I have told you."

"Yes, but as I said before, your word is much better than mine."

Her face had a stubborn, sullen cast to it. "You want me to tell others."

"It would be best if you could tell the people who uphold the law."

"Then he, Don Bonifacio, will want to know why I didn't tell the truth to begin with."

"You can tell him you were afraid to say it with your stepfather standing there. You can tell him anything for that part. But if you tell the truth about what you saw, it will be better for everyone — Ricardo's family, Carlos, even yourself."

"And my mother?"

"In the long run, yes. There is nothing stronger than the truth."

"Not even faith in God?"

"For the person whose faith is that strong, how is it different from the truth?"

She smiled. "You reason well. You could be a lawyer."

He laughed. "I am too much of an idealist. But I am also a realist in this matter. I think you can cure many ills if you tell what you know. You have seen how strong the truth is by using it to hold him in your power. But you can't go on like that forever, and you lose nothing by turning the truth over to someone else."

"Again, you reason well."

"What is your reluctance?"

She looked at the pool and then back at him. "To tell you the truth, I fear that I would be acting out of hatred if I told on him now. I have hated him, and I do not want to continue to act out of spite."

"And yet, when you hold the truth over him, is that not also out of hatred?"

"Oh, yes."

"And is there any degree to which you

might resist letting go of your power over him, just so that you may keep him twisting in pain, as you put it?"

She looked down. "There might be."

"Then which is worse, to conceal the truth or let it out?"

A smile played across her lips. "Such a lawyer."

"Let me put it another way. What would your father have you do?"

She raised her head. "My father would have had him dispatched long ago, but you are right. In these circumstances, he would say to reveal the truth."

"Do you think you can?"

After a few seconds of delay she said, "Yes, I think I can. And I will hope it helps me get over my hatred."

On the plain once again on his way back to town, Devon looked out upon the landscape as it stretched away in all directions. This was the world, and every person had a chance at it. The rule that eventually became familiar was that each person got one chance; he got to go through it only once, and whatever he made of it was his. In Devon's own life he had had, at times, the illusion that he could start over, but he knew that life went on in only one direction. And when one person's life stopped, like Ricardo's, the rest of life went on, like the Sunday *paseo*.

As he rode beneath the broad, endless sky, he had the definite sense that life was coming to a big junction for the three main inhabitants of Rancho Agua Prieta. If life had ever been innocent there, it was going to be much less so in very little time. How things played out depended on where Don Felipe had ridden off to. The best thing he could do, for his own self-preservation, would be to keep on riding — south, to Chihuahua, Durango, Zacatecas. The worse he could do would be to come back to the rancho, insist that he was still the master, act as if nothing untoward had ever happened, and continue with his old maneuvers. He was probably on some middle course, as Petra had suggested — talking to bankers and lawyers, trusting that his problems were still domestic only, and trying to find a way to bring his wife and stepdaughter into an uneasy compliance, even as he admitted, without saying it, that he had been caught with *las manos en la masa* — with his hands in the dough.

At some point before long, however, he was going to have to confront his other transgression, which he probably thought

259

he was still keeping at bay. If he had the slightest idea of what Devon and Petra had talked about at the edge of the dark pool, he would no doubt be riding straight for the Republic, perhaps after a stop at the bank.

Devon looked around at the landscape again. Off to his left about a mile, a herd of sheep lay like a dirty gray patch on a hillside. Life crawled on in the form of placid sheep out making money for the master, wherever he was. Devon hoped he didn't meet Alfonso, much less Don Felipe, on the way into town. Nevertheless, he was determined that if he did, he would not change his mission. Petra would not go to the sheriff herself, and it had to be done.

Still, Don Felipe was out there somewhere, no doubt brooding more than he was repenting. A horseman and a man of honor indeed, hoping not to have to answer for killing a man, and hoping he might have the chance after all to seduce his stepdaughter. Devon had no doubt he would see the man again. He just wondered where.

When he had ridden more than half the way back to town, Devon saw three riders appear on the trail ahead of him. They were traveling in a bunch, neither abreast nor in single file, until the distance between him and them came down to about a quarter of a mile. Then the other men came to a stop and drew up alongside one another to form a barrier of three across. Devon rode straight ahead to meet them.

As he rode the last hundred yards, he got a better view of the men. The one in the middle was older, graying and paunchy, while the other two looked as if they could be his sons. Devon recalled the inn-keeper's warning and Alfonso's lookout. These could well be Ricardo's people.

He came to a stop about five yards from the men, noticing as he did so that they had the sun at their back and were all wearing pistols. The man in the middle, who had a gray mustache and chin beard, reminded Devon in a vague way of the miniature of Petra's father. Devon placed him at about fifty-five and the two younger men in their mid-twenties. All three of them were wearing clean trousers, jackets, and hats, and their saddles were in good condition.

"Good afternoon," he called out.

The older man returned the greeting and then asked, "Where are you going?" He used the familiar form of address, and his tone made it almost a challenge.

"To town."

"And where do you come from?"

"Rancho Agua Prieta. My name is Devon Frost. I am a visiting artist."

The man nodded, and it looked as if his mustache raised and his nostrils flared. "My name is Francisco Vega Orozco. These are my sons with me."

Devon nodded to each side. The young men had full dark mustaches and dark eyes, and they bore the same unhappy expression. Returning to the father, he said, in the formal mode of address, "May I help you in some way?"

"Maybe so. If you have been to the rancho, perhaps you know where Felipe Torres can be found."

Devon relaxed his features. "I don't know. I was visiting at the house, with Doña Emilia and the señorita Petra, but Don Felipe was not there. I understood that he left for some place, but I don't know where."

"And the foreman? This fellow Alfonso?"

"I imagine he's out on the *llano* someplace. I saw him this morning when I was on my way to the old church. They have given me permission to study it for the purpose of making pictures."

"Yeh, yeh. That is well known." The man looked to each side and said, "We are here on serious business. I imagine you have heard of the great wrong that was done to our family."

"Yes, and I have sympathy for you in your sorrow."

"And we are not satisfied with how it has been handled. We take it as an affront."

Devon, feeling that his expression of sympathy was being dismissed, said, "It is well known."

The older man's face stiffened, and his eyes narrowed. "I don't suppose you know anything yourself."

"Only what I've heard, and you have no doubt heard the same things."

"You do not know much of Don Felipe, then?"

"He has not taken me into his confidence. I was present when he spoke to the sheriff, Don Bonifacio, but I am sure you know all of that."

"Oh, yes, including the daughter's testimony."

"The stepdaughter."

"It is said that Don Felipe likes to fold the blankets many times." Don Francisco raised his head and, still using the familiar forms, added, "You, who know them and who were there when the sheriff came, do you think she lied to protect him?"

Devon felt something kick inside, but he just shook his head. "She has no motive to protect him."

"Well, we know this: Ricardo left for Rancho Agua Prieta that night, with her encouragement, and he died for it. If they say he never got there, we have reason to doubt it."

"It is not my place to take Don Felipe's side, and I would not be disposed to do so anyway. But I will say this in defense of the señorita Cantera. She is very much Don Vicente's daughter."

"May he rest in peace," said Don Francisco, as if he had an obligation to say it. "But my interest is in his successor. You can't tell me where he is?"

"No, I don't know. But I assure you he was not at the house when I left there half an hour ago, and I understood that they did not expect him back soon."

Don Francisco looked at his sons again. "Well, we won't keep you any longer. Who knows where he is, or his foreman either."

"Do you have the makings for a cigarette?"

The older man frowned and then gestured to the son on his left, who dug into his jacket pocket.

"Oh, no, not for me," Devon said. "But I met a sheepherder the other day, and if you stop to ask him questions, he may ask you for the makings."

"Oh, to hell with the sheepherders! They'll lie like all the rest."

Devon shrugged. "Just a thought. But he is out in the direction where Don Felipe may have gone. Not this first herd, but another, farther out." He pointed to the south.

"Many thanks." The older man reined his horse aside, as did the son on his left, and the three of them were set to take off. They didn't seem to be very worried about trespassing on Don Felipe's land.

"May everything go well for you," Devon said.

"Likewise." And the three riders took off on a lope.

Devon watched the dust rise in their wake. Maybe this would be the easiest solution, if they got to Don Felipe first and settled things in the old way, but Devon didn't think it was the best. For one, he thought it would be better if the truth came out first; and for another, he didn't think they deserved to take things into their own hands quite so soon. Furthermore, he didn't like the way Don Francisco made his comment about Petra. Devon was convinced that she had not lied to protect Don Felipe, and he was convinced that she hadn't given him any encouragement to fold the blanket. That was a truth worth bringing out, also. He wished he'd thought to mention it to her in that way, but if it got done, she would see it and be glad of it. At least things were in motion, and he didn't mind having sent the three surly horsemen on a long ride.

CHAPTER THIRTEEN

Devon found the sheriff in the same place and in the same posture he had left him in that morning, and although he assumed Don Bonifacio had gone out somewhere that day, the identical scene made for an entertaining illusion.

"Yes, sir," said the sheriff. "Come in and have a seat."

Devon put his hand on the back of the chair he had sat in earlier, moved it a couple of feet closer to the desk, and sat down. As he did so, he took off his hat. Then he said, "I may have learned something of interest."

"Pertaining to — ?"

Devon looked at the open doorway leading to the jail cells. "The death of Ricardo Vega."

The sheriff's eyes opened. "Is that so?"

"Yes." Devon glanced again at the doorway.

"Go ahead and tell me. Don't be afraid."

"Very well. I was told, in a very credible way, that Don Felipe shot him four times that same night, not very far from the house on Rancho Agua Prieta."

"And who told you this?"

"The señorita Cantera, the person who saw it."

The sheriff put the fingertips of his two hands together. "So she has reversed her testimony. You yourself were there the first time she spoke about the incident."

"Yes."

"Well, on one of the two occasions, she is lying." He brought his hands down and set them on the desk in front of him.

"I would say it was the first time."

"And why would she have done it then?"

"I cannot speak for her, of course, but it may be that she was afraid of him."

The sheriff leaned forward. "And why would she change her mind?"

"Perhaps her desire to have the truth known has grown stronger than her fear."

"Or maybe she just wants to see the man disgraced and punished."

"I doubt it. I found her account convincing, and I believe you will, too."

"And Don Felipe, was he sitting by eating grapes while she told you this?"

"No, he was gone."

"I would think so. She talks behind his back. She throws the stone and then hides her hand."

"Well, sir, I come to you in good faith, in hopes that you will be willing to consider new evidence."

"If such it is. Do you think he is back at the rancho by now?"

"I have no way of knowing, but I was given the idea that he had ridden off and might not be back right away."

"Oh, then there's no need for me to go out there until tomorrow. I'll want to ask them both at the same time." He waved his hand. "Maybe not in the same room, but on the same trip."

Devon heard the clunk of a bucket, but from where he sat he could see only a few feet into the hallway. "In seriousness, I think it would be advisable to try to do something tonight."

"Why the hurry?"

"Well, as you may have heard, Ricardo's father and brothers are not satisfied, and they are now looking for Don Felipe. They seem to be inclined to settle things in the old way."

"Oh, yes. They're an impulsive bunch."

"But don't you see the urgency?"

Don Bonifacio shook his head. "Not as

much as you do. But look, young man. Here you have a young woman who either lied to protect her stepfather after she inspired the young man to come, or who is now lying in order to put a rope around the amorous stepfather's neck. Either way, her motive is not pure. Furthermore, I have not dismissed the possibility that her cousin Carlos might have done for young Vega. So the urgency is not strong to me."

"And Ricardo's family?"

"If Don Felipe is gone somewhere, they will have a hard time finding him, just as I would. I can go out to the rancho tomorrow, and if Don Felipe is there, we'll see if the girl holds to her story."

"Then nothing can be done right now."

The sheriff frowned and shook his head. "That's not true. There are things you can do."

"For example?"

"Entertain yourself. Distract yourself in the ways you have learned to do in this town. Don't get worked up about other people's problems."

Devon rose with his hat in his hand. "Thank you for your attention."

"To the contrary. Thank you for your information."

On his way out, Devon tried to catch a

better glimpse of the hallway and jail area. He saw no one, but he had a good hunch that someone had been eavesdropping.

Devon sat by himself once again in the quiet dining room. He felt the presence of the Virgin of Guadalupe, benevolent as always, radiant from her place on the wall. Beyond the light of the two oil lamps, the pale bird made its clucking noise and small shifting sounds in its cage in the corner. Federico served the evening meal — a platter of beans, rice, chunks of pork, and green chile, plus a stack of corn tortillas. Seven o'clock was a normal time for Devon to have his evening meal, but knowing as he did that the townspeople took their main meal in the early afternoon and usually had something light in the evening, he felt like the boarder who worked late and had to have supper set aside for him. Nevertheless, even if the food had been sitting in the kitchen for a few hours, it came to the table hot, and it tasted good.

The lodging itself had been a dependable, constant feature in his stay so far. Now that he thought of it, off to himself, he realized that the church and the rancho had changed in his experience of them. On his last visit, the church had assumed the identity of an old crumbling set of walls; at least for the time being, it had lost its aura or inherent character. The rancho, likewise, did not feel like the stately remnant of a once-glorious hacienda but rather a piece of trodden property that Don Felipe and Alfonso rode over and that Ricardo and his family trespassed upon.

Maybe it was time to leave, he thought. The charm had worn thin; tradition had been brought down to the level of sheep hooves. Yet, when he thought of Doña Emilia and Petra, he felt that all was not lost. The swineherds had not taken over the palace, and grace had not been dragged through the dirt. No, it was more like the old plays in which a bad king had to be gotten rid of.

He brought his own thoughts back to earth. Too much fanciful thinking, he told himself. Better to focus on what he could do, for the benefit of Petra and Carlos — and Doña Emilia as well, although she was the one who would suffer the most, no matter which way things fell.

That was it, focus on what he could do, which was next to nothing. He knew what needed to be done — bring things from the dark into the light — but he didn't feel he had accomplished much with the sheriff so far. For the rest of the evening, about all he could do was to keep his eyes and ears open, at least for a short space of time. He looked at his plate and recalled the sheriff's recommendation, which in spite of its sarcasm had some validity. The food at Los Ermitaños was good, but it always left him wanting a beer or two.

Night had just fallen when Devon walked into La Sombra, but a good crowd of patrons had already gathered. Alfonso stood with his group of hangerson, and as Devon walked past them, he sensed an attitude among them, as if they were in the know, close to people who ran things, while everyone else was common rabble. A short quip from Alfonso brought out a chorus of laughter attended by knowing smiles.

Devon found a place farther down the bar, where Lalo served him a glass of beer as he lapsed into his own company. Juanito, another day further from his last shave and bath, was singing his *corrido* about the young suitor who was killed in the moonlight. His soul, turned into a pigeon, sang from the bell tower of the church.

Cu-ru-cu, cu-ru-cu-cu, so sings the sad
   lover,

Who died in the moonlight surprised and
   alone.
Cu-ru-cu, cu-ru-cu-cu, so sings the lone
   pigeon,
Who waits for the day when the truth will
   be known.

Alfonso did not sing along with this song,
so his group of sycophants didn't either.
But the foreman had a smug look on his
face as he nodded to the rhythm and built a
cornhusk cigarette.

A couple of songs later, Juanito played a
piece that Devon hadn't heard before. His
attention was drawn to it because Alfonso
and his group perked up when the song
started. It was a *corrido* also, a stilted ballad
about a woman referred to as *la malquerida,*
the wrongly loved one. It had a faster tempo
than the song about the dead suitor, and
Juanito took flamboyant strokes on his
instrument as he grimaced and cried out
the words. Apparently he had played the
song before, perhaps more than once, for
Alfonso and his followers joined in when
Juanito come to the chorus.

Oh, he pursued her in the night time,
He pursued her in the day,
And this wrongly loved young woman

274

Couldn't keep his love at bay,
For his passion hot and pointed,
Like a pair of silver spurs,
Urged him onward in his conquest
As he pressed his will to hers.

Alfonso's silver tooth flashed as he sang along, and all the men in his group raised their glasses.

Two slouching figures drifted along the bar and moved into the light of an overhead lantern. Devon recognized the long features of Cayetano and the bearded face of the sheriff's lackey. From the way that Cayetano averted his eyes and then recovered, Devon guessed that the man knew of Devon's most recent conversation with Don Bonifacio. In another moment, Cayetano had resumed his usual demeanor and came sidling in his obsequious way.

"*Buenas noches, jefe.*"

"*Buenas noches.*"

"It is a good way to pass the evening, after a long day's work. I assume you worked today, as always. You are very attentive to your duty."

"I made some drawings with a pencil, but I do not feel that I did a day's work."

"I know you worked. For that you deserve to relax, to rest."

Devon said nothing in response.

"I know also," the man resumed, "that it is difficult for me to tell you something you don't already know. Otherwise, I would offer to share what little I know."

Devon shrugged. "It seems as if very little is worth knowing."

"There is a saying, that he who knows much is not the wise man, but rather he who knows the important things."

"Would that I were either of those two."

"On the contrary, I believe you are both."

"I try not to fool people, but I may have done so with you, without trying."

"Oh, come on, *jefe.* You are too modest. But it goes well with your generosity."

"And my fame."

Cayetano gave him a sly look. "I would not impose upon your generosity if I thought you knew where Don Felipe is, or why Ricardo's father and brothers are out riding."

"Indeed?"

"Yes, and in truth, it hurts me to suggest it."

"Suggest what?"

"The little cooperation. I would not want you to think that it is more important to me than your friendship."

Devon gave him a ten-cent piece. "Here. I

have a reputation for generosity to uphold."

"Thank you. Your reputation is well deserved." The coin disappeared. "As for Don Felipe, he went out but he did not go away. This is what I have heard from someone who saw him coming back."

"Does the sheriff know this?"

"He does not value my knowledge, so I do not offer it on my own."

"I think he is deeper than he seems." Devon raised his eyebrows.

"Like a duck."

"Like a duck?"

"Yes, the little pot for boiling water for tea. It is called a *pato.*"

"Another thing for me to learn. I will have a veritable treasure when I leave Tinaja."

"Which, we hope, will not happen soon."

"Very well." Devon took a drink of beer. "What else?"

"I'm sure you already know that they buried Ricardo today."

"No, I didn't know that."

"A small thing."

"In the life of his family, quite large."

"Without a doubt. I give it a little importance now so that a person might understand."

"Understand what?"

"Now that the funeral is over, his father

and brothers have saddled their horses."

"That doesn't surprise me."

"I didn't think it would." Cayetano smiled in a self-satisfied expression. "You came into town a little while after they left, but I doubted that either they or the sheriff would tell you about the funeral."

"None of them did."

"And it is useful to know that they don't have anything holding them back now."

Devon hunched his shoulders. "They're not looking for me."

Cayetano resembled a stone figure as he said, "No, but for your own reasons, you care about what happens to Don Felipe." Then with half a bow of false servitude he said, *"Gracias, jefe,"* and turned away. He and his bearded friend went to the far end of the bar, near the door, and summoned the bartender.

Devon turned so that he did not have to see them anymore. For as much as he found his conversation with Cayetano distasteful, he had to admit that one reason for coming to the cantina was to pick up information, and he knew he wasn't going to get it from Alfonso.

The foreman and his pals were still whooping it up. Juanito was singing the song about the man who went from town to town, from cantina to cantina, knew all the night-time ladies and deflowered many girls. Alfonso was singing along and gyrating with his hips, much to the amusement of the others in his group.

Devon shifted to stare at his glass again. It seemed as if all the loafers and moochers and gossipers had come out tonight, waiting for something to happen. He looked up and down the bar. It was human nature. These men were no different from the ones he had known in Ohio, Pennsylvania, or Illinois. If one man dragged another out into the street and cursed him in the most indiscreet terms, a crowd of men would gather to gawk and listen. The same happened if there was a fire or a drowning. No matter how personal or how unfortunate the event, it always drew an audience.

The chatter and the laughter went on, with Juanito's music blended in. With some songs, no one paid attention as he stood, blank-faced, and hurled his verses out into the air. With other selections, the patrons sang along and brought life to Juanito's face, and his broad stare resembled that of a man with sight.

Now he sang again about the *malquerida*. *Oh, she's the wrongly loved one, and she knows that it's a sin.*

Alfonso held his drink aloft and did a high-stepping figure-eight.

He's the one who loves her wrongly, and he can't sleep at night.

Alfonso took another turn, and his boon companions stood by, clapping.

Juanito went into the chorus, and half the men in the cantina sang along.

> Oh, he pursued her in the night time,
> He pursued her in the day,
> And this wrongly loved young woman
> Couldn't keep his love at bay,
> For his passion hot and pointed,
> Like a pair of silver spurs,
> Urged him onward in his conquest
> As he pressed his will to hers.

A few at a time, the men's voices died away, and Juanito was left singing by himself. Still animated, he went through the chorus again.

Devon followed the glances of some of the men and saw that the front door of the cantina stood open. In the dark of the doorway, beyond the lamplight, a tall figure in black stood in profile, showing his left side. He wore black trousers and a black jacket, embroidered in his recognizable style, and he held his head at an angle so that the wide-brimmed sombrero shaded his face from view. Then, as if he had practiced it a thousand times, he turned his head upward and around, and the brim of the sombrero lifted to show the hard cheekbones and angry dark eyes of Don Felipe Torres.

He strode into the cantina, his spurs clinking, as Juanito continued to sing about the *malquerida.*

Devon looked around for Alfonso, but the foreman was nowhere to be seen. Devon glanced at the back door, which told no tales.

Don Felipe walked up to the singer, who still seemed to be gazing out at his audience. With his left hand the master batted the mandolin upward and snatched the man's shirtfront. With his right hand he slapped the blind man's face back and forth, and then, as if he finally saw the emptiness in the man's eyes, he froze with his hand uplifted. He relaxed his grip and lowered his right hand, reached into his pocket and drew out a coin, and pressed it into the singer's hand.

By now, all other noise in the cantina had died to nothing, and the master's voice carried as he said to the singer, "Make fun of me as you will. But I will yet make her mine." Then, sweeping the place with a contemptuous glance, he strode to the door. His clinking spurs made the only sound in the cantina even as he tossed a coin to Lalo the bartender. He did not close the door behind him, and a few seconds later the hoofbeats of a fast horse pounded in the street.

Lalo called across the barroom. "Are you all right, Juanito?"

Juanito spoke in a clear, steady voice. "Oh, yes. Once he came close enough, I would have known him from the perfumed smell, even if he hadn't spoken. Thanks to God, he is gone. The master of the rancho is in a hurry to go for his *malquerida*."

The tension in the air broke and fell into a dozen pieces, one man muttering to another. Then, with no mercy, Juanito resumed the song about the *malquerida*.

He's the one who loves her wrongly, and he can't sleep at night.

A few men started clapping, a few more joined in, and at least two or three were stomping their feet. Through the noise came the ringing sound of one spurred boot heel.

Time to go, Devon thought. *Leave this saloon, leave this town, leave this antiquated world with its sawdust-filled, strutting lord.*

As he turned to set his glass on the bar, he saw a full one in front of him. Down the bar, Lalo was pouring tequila into a row of glasses held by the outstretched hands of four or five patrons. Devon gave a questioning look to the man standing next to him.

"Una ronda," said the man. A round.

A round on the house, Devon assumed. That was the time-honored method to get the crowd settled. He shrugged and took a drink. No hurry. The storm had passed. The cantina shrank back into its own little world, and someone, mindful of keeping peace with the town, had shut the door.

A few minutes later, the front door burst open and two men strode in. As they came into the lamplight, Devon recognized them as Ricardo's brothers. They were dressed as they had been earlier in the day, in neat, clean riding outfits and round-brimmed hats. Spurs jingled as the two men came to the edge of the open area in the middle of the room, and with thumbs in their cartridge belts they moved their heads back and forth as they searched the place.

Lalo, who had brought a glass of beer to Juanito, called across to them. "What do you want?"

"We're looking for Felipe Torres," said the one who looked as if he might be the older.

Juanito, holding the glass of beer at chest level, had half a sneer as he piped up. "He has gone back to the rancho to be with his *malquerida.* He does not give up, even when the female dog sits on her tail. Who are you?" Like Lalo, he addressed them in the plural.

"Brothers of Ricardo Vega."

For the second time in less than a quarter of an hour, the place went dead quiet. Devon took a drink from his beer and studied the two brothers. From their expression, he figured they had heard the gossip about Petra seeing the murder. They looked harder and more resolute than they had been earlier in the day.

"Have a drink," said Juanito. "Lalo is treating everyone to a round."

"Not exactly," said the barkeep. "Don Felipe paid for the round on his way out."

A ripple of laughter went around the cantina. Of course, thought Devon. Juanito hadn't seen it, but he had, and he didn't register it. A round on Rancho Agua Prieta.

"No, thanks," said the brother. "We have to go find our father." The two men turned and walked out of the saloon, spurs jingling, and again someone closed the door.

When the hoofbeats died away, Devon made his way out of the cantina. For all he knew, Cayetano would finish the half-glass of beer he had left. He didn't care.

Once he was outside in the clear air, he did not feel so fed up with this whole world. Tinaja filled in around him, a decent little town where the gnarled old widow could walk without harm in the main street and where a man with a load of sticks could water his burro in the public trough. As for the coarse humor in La Sombra, he could find that sort of thing, and the swaggering, in other places. If it hadn't been for his personal acquaintance with Petra and Doña Emilia, very little of it would have gotten under his skin.

He looked up at the stars. It was good to be outside where he could clear his thoughts. The Vega brothers, once they found their father, would not wait until morning as the sheriff had said he would do. They would go to the rancho and call out Don Felipe in front of the family and servants. For as much as Devon thought the master might deserve that kind of showdown, Doña Emilia didn't. The original inhabitants of Rancho Agua Prieta had not lost their civility because of the man who had come to live there; and as a matter of principle, the process of the law should take precedence over the old ways of the Vega family.

Standing under the wide sky, Devon re-

alized he had helped send Ricardo's kins-
men to the rancho. That meant one thing.
He couldn't go back to his room, get a
night's sleep, and find out in the morning
what had happened — not after having
spilled the beans. He owed it to Doña
Emilia and Petra, and maybe by some
stretch Don Felipe, to get a horse and ride
out there tonight.

CHAPTER FOURTEEN

The moon hung high and bright, a couple of nights past the full moon, so Devon felt he was up to the task of making a fast ride across the plain. The trail would look different at night, but he knew it well enough. Don Felipe would have arrived at the rancho a ways ahead of him, and Alfonso might have gotten there as well. The main hazard, other than the horse taking a spill, was the chance that he might cross paths with or be pursued by Ricardo's people before he made it to the rancho.

Devon rousted the stableman, who came to the door barefoot and wrapped in a serape. When Devon told him what he needed, the man complained that it was way too early, but as Devon persisted, the man said he would be back in a moment. A few minutes later he reappeared, dressed in his work clothes and carrying a lantern. In another ten minutes he had Devon's horse ready to go.

As he handed the reins to Devon in the lamp-lit stable, he said, "Something in earnest would help me not worry about letting a horse go in the middle of the night. Anything could happen."

Devon winced as he imagined breaking his neck or getting a bullet through the ribs. "Take this," he said, giving the man a ten-dollar gold piece. "We'll settle the account later."

"Very well, sir." The stableman opened the door. "I hope everything goes well for you."

"Thank you." Devon led the horse out into the moonlight, checked the cinch, and stepped into the saddle. He let the animal walk to the edge of town, to warm it up and to get out of earshot of the sleeping townspeople. Then he touched his heel to the flank, and the horse went into a lope.

Devon could feel that his recent riding stood him in good stead. His balance and his riding legs fit right into place, and he felt in harmony with the animal as it covered the ground. The trail was not hard to follow, and the horse knew it anyway, so the country flowed by. In the cool of the night, Devon could smell the dry grass and dust and the warm, sweetish odor of the horse.

The rancho did not come into view quite as soon as he expected, but the trail was true and the horse was dependable, and finally the adobe wall and the stone gateway appeared in the moonlight about half a mile ahead. As he peered in the night, he made out the darker shapes of the trees, taller on the left side than on the right.

He followed the trail right up to the gate, which, to his surprise, stood partway open. Having slowed the horse to a walk, he reined it left and then right to weave through the gateway. Just as he was straightening the animal out, an unseen force slammed the free end of the gate into the front shoulder of the horse, which lurched sideways and backwards. Devon lost his right stirrup and began to slip to the left, so rather than take a fall, he grabbed the saddle horn with both hands, kicked his feet free, and pushed backwards. He landed on his feet with the left rein still in his grasp.

A coarse voice came from the shadows of the trees on the other side of the gateway. "Who goes there?"

"It is I, the artist."

"Beggar," said the other man. As he stepped forward from the shadows, his pale hat shone in the moonlight, which also cast a sheen on the leather vest.

"Alfonso," said Devon, "there's not any time to lose."

The foreman laid his left hand on the headstall of Devon's horse. "You presume too much," he said, with a slur that Devon could now detect.

"Look, I didn't come to fight. I came to warn Don Felipe."

"He doesn't need your help." With his hand still on the bridle, Alfonso stepped in front of the horse and pushed his chest out. "And who's to say you won't fight?" Letting go of the headstall, he stepped forward and with both hands shoved Devon backwards.

Devon could smell liquor on the man's breath, and although the shove was forceful, it was clumsy. Devon stumbled backward, letting go of the rein, and then regained his footing.

Alfonso took another step forward and swung out his right arm in an attempt to grab Devon by the shirtfront.

Devon batted the hand away and got into a better stance. "Look," he said, "don't be so difficult."

Alfonso lunged forward in an apparent move to grab a hold, but Devon stepped back and aside. Alfonso stumbled, straightened up, turned, and rushed again.

Devon smelled liquor and sweat as the

man closed in on him. Devon was reluctant to throw the first punch and turn things into a fistfight, so he ducked and grabbed Alfonso's right leg. Then he stood up and away, holding his opponent's leg by the calf and boot heel. Alfonso hopped on his left foot to try to keep balance until Devon stepped forward, planted his right foot behind the other man's heel, gave the uplifted leg a slight turn, and sent Alfonso falling back onto his butt.

Devon stepped past him and his fallen hat, lingering just long enough to make sure the man wasn't drawing a pistol, and gathered the reins of his horse. He swung aboard and moved forward at a trot, across the parade ground in the moonlight. Horses came to the openings in their stalls, and a couple of them nickered. Devon saw two white heads peering out, and he figured one of the animals had just been put away.

Up to the hitching rail, he made a fast dismount and tied his horse. As he made his way to the door of the *portal,* which was ajar, he heard raised voices from within the house. He stood for a moment, trying to pick up words and identify who said them, and suddenly the door jerked open and Don Felipe stood there.

He was still in full regalia, from his sombrero and embroidered jacket down to his pistol and black trousers. As he stepped through the doorway and drew the pistol, his spurs clinked. Devon figured the man had left the argument inside the house and had come as quietly as he could to see if someone had come into the yard.

"You!" said Don Felipe, with his eyes glaring. "What in the devil do you want?"

Devon did not move, and so he made it easy for the master of the rancho to grab a handful of his shirt. Nevertheless, he held his chin up firm and said, "I came to warn you."

"You came to stick your nose in," said Don Felipe, laying the end of his pistol barrel between Devon's cheekbone and nose.

"I know you don't like me, but —"

With his left hand, the master shook Devon's upper body. "I don't like! No, I don't. Not at all. I've never liked you being around my daughter."

Devon tipped his head back. He had the feeling that Don Felipe had latched onto him as a way to reassert his authority, more of an exercise than a deadly grudge. Nevertheless, a pistol barrel was something serious. "I did not come with that interest," he said.

At that moment Doña Emilia appeared at

the doorway and stepped through, with Consuelo following her and carrying a lantern. "What is the matter?" asked the lady. Then she said, "Oh, the artist. Let him go, Felipe. He doesn't do us any harm."

"I don't like him."

"Let him go. He has always come here as a friend, in confidence."

Don Felipe lowered his pistol, and Devon was able to nod to Emilia, who, in a white blouse and black sweater, looked pale and worried in the lantern light.

"*Buenas noches, señor artista.*"

"*Buenas noches, señora.*"

The taller man released his grasp on Devon's shirt and, holstering his pistol, stood back a step. Before anyone had a chance to speak again, Petra came through the doorway and made a petulant halt.

"What is this?" she demanded. "What are you doing?" Devon noticed that she used the familiar form of address with her stepfather, which went along with her insolent tone.

Don Felipe tipped his head to one side, and without turning to look at her he said, "Your lukewarm admirer has come on some business not yet made clear."

"You beast!" she spat out, her face hardening in contempt. "You can't live with the idea that anyone else might have a normal relation, while you, with your sick passion, make your attempts while my mother is under the same roof! In the next room, and you, conceited as a cat, expecting to have your way."

The master tipped his head again and wrinkled his nose, as if he was trying to deflect the tirade with his shoulder. Devon had the impression that Petra was either repeating or restating what she had been saying inside and possibly what she had said earlier in the day, and again, she seemed to be delivering it for an audience.

"House of my mother," she went on. "And you with your whispered words."

"Enough," said Doña Emilia. "The artist has come here for some reason, not to listen to this."

Petra smiled to him, though her eyes were still narrowed in anger. "Welcome," she said.

"Thank you." Devon had stood back a couple of steps and was smoothing his shirt.

"Give him a chance to speak," said Doña Emilia, still in her placating tone.

Devon took a deep breath and released it as he pulled himself up straight. "I came to warn Don Felipe that Ricardo's people are looking for him and are probably coming this way."

"Tonight?" said Doña Emilia, her voice rising. "Why now?"

Devon looked at Petra, and finding no resistance there, turned to her mother. "It is known that Ricardo met his death here."

Don Felipe cut in. "It is said. Many things are said."

Devon brought his glance again to Petra, to imply that it was her turn.

"The artist is right," she said, in a steady voice. "It is known."

Don Felipe gave her a look of surprise and recognition mixed, but he said nothing.

After a few seconds of silence, Emilia spoke. "If the artist is not mistaken, that they may be on their way —"

"Let them come." The master gave a toss of his sombreroed head, and the lantern light glanced off his high cheekbone. "Sheep shearers. Hog butchers that smell of lard."

"Felipe —"

"Let them come." Then, as if he had finally regained the authority he had been trying to assert, he said, "Go inside. Both of you. If they come, this is no place for women." Don Felipe took out a cigarette, lit it, and shook out the match.

Emilia gave him a critical look, then turned and went in through the *portal* with Consuelo behind her. Petra followed with a lighter step, swishing her dress and making a cheerful silhouette in the yellow light.

When the lantern went away, the area outside came back into focus in the moonlight. With no one speaking, Devon felt that he and Don Felipe were both listening for the drumming of hooves.

A movement with the scuff of a footstep sounded from the direction of the water trough. Both men turned.

"Who goes there?" called Don Felipe, not very loud but in his commanding tone.

"Just me," came the dull voice of Alfonso.

"Why aren't you at the gate?"

"I came to see if you needed help."

"You think I need help with this?"

"I didn't know. I heard several voices."

"Everyone hears a great deal." Don Felipe took an imperious puff on his cigarette and turned to Devon. "And you?"

"I suppose I said what I came here to say."

"More than enough."

"And with no other motive, I can go back to town."

"May you have a safe trip."

Devon noted the formal usage. "Thank you," he said. "Good night."

He walked to his horse in the moonlight, untied him, and gathered the reins. As he turned the horse around and got ready to mount, he realized he heard a low, rumbling sound. He stopped and listened. It sounded like a small of group of horses running together.

Devon looked around at Don Felipe, who stood up straight with his head lifted and turned to one side, the glowing end of his cigarette at chest height.

From the sound of it, the horses were getting closer.

"Alfonso," called the master. "Is the gate closed?"

"No, this one left it opened."

"This one." After a few seconds, Don Felipe spoke again, in the tone he used with Devon. "You. Don't leave yet, until we see what it is."

Devon waited, listening out into the night. Alfonso and Don Felipe both seemed poised as well.

"Alfonso, go to the gate. No, wait. I think they are too close. Aren't they?"

"I think so."

"Damn them. Let them come." Don Felipe dropped his cigarette and stepped on it, then drew his pistol and, holding it down by his side, walked out onto the parade ground to stand in the moonlight.

Devon, at the edge of the shadow near the building, grabbed the reins of his horse up close to the bit with his right hand and held the slack ends in his left. With any commotion, he would want to have a good grip on the horse.

The hoofbeats thudded louder now. The riders came in through the gate, past the pool and the cottonwoods, and across the hard ground. They drew rein in front of the man on the ground. Devon could smell dust and the warmth of horses as the dark animals bunched and settled. He counted the riders — one, two, three. Then he recognized the voice of Ricardo's father.

"Felipe!"

"Here I am."

"This, for my son!"

Gunfire flamed as a pistol shot rang out. Don Felipe's form jerked as he hunched over. The gun-man's horse jumped to the left as the man, leaning out, pointed and fired again. Don Felipe fell to the ground on all fours as his sombrero spilled off to the side. The elder Vega rode in a circle around him, closing off Devon's view, and the two sons fell in behind him in single file, riding in a circle and firing at the man on the ground. After about eight shots, they broke file and galloped off in a bunch, slowing at the gate and then pounding away out onto the plain.

Devon's horse, meanwhile, was pulling backwards and thrashing from one side to the other, so Devon had to grab and pull hard. When he got the animal settled down, he turned his attention back to the scene of the shooting. He could see that the master of the rancho was done for, lying facedown in the dirt, a dark form in the moonlight. He could also see the foreman, who had hung back and watched from a safe spot behind the stone water tank.

Alfonso took slow steps out into the open and stopped about ten yards from the body. He stood, not weaving and not still, and he looked as if he was in a stupor.

The door of the *portal* flung open, and Doña Emilia, dressed in the same black and white, came rushing out and crying.

Consuelo followed at a fast walk, carrying the lantern. She caught up with Emilia, who stood over the body and sobbed. "Oh, my God, help us God. What has happened?"

As the lady knelt by her dead husband, Petra came out into the yard, taking slow, deliberate steps.

Miguel appeared from somewhere out of the shadows by the carriage room, and two of the men Devon had seen hanging around the gate now emerged from the area of the bunkhouse.

No one spoke for a few minutes as the woman sobbed and cried. Then she stood up, with the help of Consuelo lifting her at the elbow. With the dignity of a queen rising from a fallen king, she turned to her daughter and said, loud enough for the others to hear, "I cannot help it. I know what he was, but he is still my husband. We will sit up with the body, and we will bury him with the honor that the master of Rancho Agua Prieta deserves." With tearfilled eyes she looked around at the rest, and then she went into the house. Consuelo walked at her side, an arm around her shoulders in consolation.

Alfonso stepped forward, pulled his hat down onto his brow, and barked at the two men from the bunkhouse. "Go for blankets and a litter, and carry him into the house."

The two hired men, who seemed to be relieved to have something to do, broke away and hurried toward their quarters. Miguel muttered something and went to the house.

Devon looked across at Petra, too far away for him to see very well in the moonlight. "Shall we talk?" he said.

"Yes, we can talk."

He thought it would be best to keep his horse out of the way, so he led the animal out into the yard and past the fallen body, to a spot in the open where he waited for Petra. When she reached him, the two of them walked across the parade ground to the far end of the enclosed area. At the edge of the cottonwoods, where Devon could see the moonlight reflected on the surface of the pool, they paused.

"It all happened so fast," he said. "The Vegas came in, rode up to him, and shot him before he knew to raise his pistol. The father shot first."

"It is their way. And his, too."

"I am sorry for your mother. It was largely for her benefit that I came, but as it turned out, I came in vain."

"You tried. That counts for something."

"Yes, but the result is that your mother has to go through this ordeal, not only to lose her husband but to be present when he is killed. That is a strong blow, even if, as she says, she knows what he was."

Petra's words came out tense, as if she were speaking through clenched teeth. "It is fitting that she treat him with dignity, for, as she says, he is her husband. But I know what he was, too, and I am not obliged to honor him."

"I can see that your bitterness does not go away at once."

She took a moment to answer. "Perhaps not. But I feel that I have gotten over my hatred. That may be the only good thing that comes out of this wreckage."

"There might be something else."

"What is that?" Her silver cross flashed in the moonlight as she turned her head.

"You still have the opportunity to clarify the truth about Ricardo's death."

She looked at the ground. "Does it matter much, except to show that the Vegas had justification?"

Devon hesitated a couple of seconds. "I think the Vegas knew that you were ready to tell the sheriff, just as the sheriff did."

"I see. Then you spoke with him already."

"Yes."

"Then what is the other good?"

"You have the chance to show that you weren't lying to protect this man. It would be much worse if people were to go on thinking that you had that motive."

"Is that what they think?"

"Some do."

"Well, thank you. I might not have thought about that right away."

"The sheriff, according to him, was going to come out tomorrow morning. Now he will have two reasons. Meanwhile, it's good to be prepared as things come to a resolution."

"I appreciate it." After a moment of silence, she spoke again. "And yourself? Does any of this affect you?"

"Of course, all of it does in the sense that it has helped me to understand your way of life here. But as for my work, which I think is what you probably mean, I believe I had already reached a point there."

"Reached a point?"

"What I mean is, I think I have studied the old church enough."

"You are full up with it."

"Something like that. I feel that I have gotten as much out of it as I am going to."

"And so you will leave. You will go away."

He nodded. "I think it is time."

Her eyes roved over him. "It is not for anything we have done here?"

"Oh, no. You have treated me well, and I find both you and your mother, each in your own way, very cordial and gracious. And interesting. But I know it is going to take time for both of you to live through these things that have happened. It is not a good time to have a frequent visitor, with whatever motives, and it would not be a good reason, now, for me to stay in Tinaja."

"You may be right. My heart is cold and

closed right now."

"Things don't happen all at once," he said. "Well, some things do, like this, but other things, like problems of feeling, they take time."

"That is one more truth I have heard from you. You have not lived your few years in vain."

He smiled. "Maybe it just means I have not been very good at solving problems."

"Well," she said in a resigned tone, "you know what you must do. But when you leave, you must come here again to say farewell. It would not be good if you didn't take leave of my mother, and right now is not a good time."

"That's true. I will pass by here on my way."

CHAPTER FIFTEEN

Carlos was waiting in the reception area when Devon came down for breakfast the next morning. As he rose from his chair and stood ready to shake hands, Devon surmised the young man knew he was out of trouble. His light-brown eyes had a clear, open expression, and he was clean-shaven. Even his drooping mustache looked less mournful. He was neatly dressed as always, in a brown corduroy jacket and trousers and a clean white shirt. As he reached out his hand, Devon noticed, in addition to its not being roughened by work, a yellowish stain on the thumb and first two fingers. In spite of his fresh appearance, he had been smoking plenty of cigarettes.

As they shook hands and exchanged *"Buenos días,"* Devon invited Carlos to join him for breakfast. Once they were seated in the dining room, Carlos began the conversation with what Devon took to be his sense of appropriate form.

"I understand some notable events took place last night, and I want to thank you for your part in it all."

"I didn't do much, and I didn't succeed in getting Don Felipe to heed my warning."

"Yes, but you also took the initiative earlier. I understand you were able to get my cousin to disclose a truth that otherwise might not have come out."

Devon was gratified to know that Petra's testimony, or her willingness to give it, was now common knowledge. "Well, yes, that was a good thing, although it may have precipitated the revenge of Ricardo's family."

Carlos wagged his head in a small motion. "They might have done it anyway. After all, Don Felipe issued his death threat in the presence of both Ricardo and his father." He tipped his head again. "But this way, it is clear who did what."

"Oh, yes. It's best to have the truth out."

Federico appeared with two cups of coffee and returned to the kitchen.

"I hope it has not been too great a distraction from your work," Carlos resumed.

"Not much. I think I have achieved as much as I could expect on this visit."

"Oh, really? Are you close to finishing,

then? Will you be leaving?"

"I think so. I have to take leave of a couple of people, but otherwise there is not much to detain me here."

"I'm glad I dropped by this morning, then."

"Oh, fear not. I would have come by your house."

"That's good. And in any future time, likewise, you will always be welcome there." Carlos's eyebrows drew together in a thoughtful gesture. "Do you leave today, then? Does the coach go today?"

"Actually, it does not leave today, but rather than wait two days, I will rent a couple of horses. One for me, and one for my things."

"Oh, uh-huh."

"The coachman will bring them back on his next round."

"That's a long trip to make, alone."

Devon sensed that Carlos saw it as something that he himself would not do. "Well, I came here on my own, and I've been riding back and forth to the rancho by myself, and the horse knows me."

"Ah, that's good. And you are very competent."

Devon smiled. "At some things. I don't know if I could roll a cigarette with a cornhusk or ride a wild horse."

Carlos shrugged as he gave a casual down-turn to his mouth and a toss of his head. *"Cada chancho a su rancho."* Each pig to its own ranch. Then, in his tone of appropriate form, he said, "Do you plan to say farewell to my aunt and cousin?"

"Yes." Thinking it might help to dispel worry about the cousin, Devon added, "And to a person here in town, not to be mentioned in the same sentence, but someone who has treated me well all the same."

Carlos gave a flicker of recognition. "That is something to be missed."

"Indeed it is. As I heard once in a saying, if there are days in which the duck swims, there are others in which he doesn't even get a drink of water."

Carlos laughed. "You speak Spanish very well — too well to visit only once."

The house with no windows in front had a different cast to it in the light of mid-morning than it did on Devon's previous visits. With the sun at his back he tapped on the door frame with his penknife, and after waiting a few minutes he tapped again. At last the door opened, and the woman with the wide face and reddish hair appeared. She was wearing a housecoat that, along with the puffiness of her features, confirmed Devon's expectation that things would be moving slowly at this hour.

"What do you want?"

"Excuse me, I know it is early, but I am leaving town, and I just wanted to say good-bye to the young woman here who has been my friend."

"I don't know."

"A few minutes, nothing more, in the front room."

The madame shook her head and said again, "I don't know." She cast a glance over Devon, said, "Just a minute," and closed the door.

Devon stood warming in the sunlight. He felt conspicuous, and he thought he should feel foolish, although he didn't.

The door opened, and the madame's features presented themselves again. "Come in. But don't make much noise. The others are still sleeping."

Devon walked into the dusky parlor, where one lamp had been lit and placed on a sideboard at the end of the room. The madame closed the door behind him, crossed the room, and went into the curtained hallway. He heard her voice and another, and a few seconds later Ramona came into the room.

Like her landlady, she was wearing a housecoat with nightclothes visible at top and bottom. Her hair fell loose at her shoulders, and although she was not wearing lipstick, rouge, or earrings, her face had a rested, composed look to it, and the bronze texture of her skin was pleasing to his eye.

"Señor *artista*," she said, giving him her hand. "What is such an early visit owing to?"

"I am sorry to bother anyone, but I told you I would come by to see you before I left town, and it seems that today is the day I leave."

"Oh, that is too bad," she said, with what he thought was some degree of sincerity. "We will miss you."

"I will certainly miss you, and I will think about you often."

She half-closed her eyes as she nodded. "How nice. If you ever come this way again, you must come here — unless your company does not allow it." A restrained smile played on her face.

"Yours is the company I like the most."

"Very amiable." Her face relaxed. "Your company has been pleasant as well."

He took a breath as he put himself up to say what he had thought out. "Also on my last visit, I said I could give you my name and address on a slip of paper." He took the folded paper from his jacket pocket and handed it to her. "There is no obligation, but if you ever feel inclined to write, especially if you go back to the Republic, your correspondence would be very welcome."

"Thank you." She took the paper and without unfolding it put it in the pocket of her robe. "There is no way to predict the future."

"That's true."

"You go north, and I go south, if God pleases. You do not know what kind of life awaits me there. And here, this is how you know me." She waved her hand at the room in general.

He shrugged. "To me you are a woman more than a person in a particular line of work. Wherever I saw you again, I would be pleased. Meanwhile, you have treated me well and you have done me good. I will have fine memories of you."

"That is very good, señor *artista*. And thank you for keeping your word and coming to see me before you leave. I will not throw away your address."

She gave him her hand again and wished him a good trip, and then he was outside in the bright daylight, recognizing what a nice illusion it had been and reminding himself of the things he had yet to do.

Rancho Agua Prieta looked solid and whole as he rode up to the stone gateway. This place would go on, he told himself, prevailing from one generation to the next. For all he knew, either Doña Emilia or Petra could bring a new master to the rancho, someone with a new set of habits and preferences, but the rancho itself would maintain its character.

Alfonso was nowhere in sight as a dark man in a peaked straw hat, one of the two regulars, opened the gate and let Devon ride through. The dark pool on his left lay in the cool shadows of late morning, and the horses in the stalls looked out with curiosity at the saddle horse, which they knew, and the unfamiliar packhorse that trailed behind.

Devon rode forward, crossing the parade ground and noticing where someone had raked dirt across the spot where the body had fallen. When he lifted his eyes, he saw Petra standing in the doorway of the *portal.* He lifted his hand in greeting, then continued to the hitching rail, where he tied the two horses.

He walked toward her as she stood there,

poised. She was wearing a dark gray, full-length dress with long sleeves, which gave her a somber aspect. Her hair was not tied back as usual, but her face still held a tight expression.

"You are all ready to leave," she said as she took a couple of steps away from the doorway and into the yard.

"It's a long trip, but I can make it in one day, and I didn't have any strong reasons for staying."

She gave him her hand, ungloved. "Very good on your part to come by and take leave of us."

He took her hand and released it, noticing her little silver cross as he did so. "I couldn't have done otherwise."

She put her hands together in front of her, then turned sideways and lifted her right hand in a motion toward the door. "Come in where there is shade."

"Thank you."

He took off his hat and followed her into the *portal.* The door to the tack room was closed, but the door to the house was open, and he heard footsteps within. Then the door opened, and Doña Emilia, dressed fully in black, stepped outside. On her chest lay a silver cross bordered in black, larger than the one she usually wore.

"Oh, señor *artista,* how good of you to come. I'm afraid we haven't been very good to you." In spite of her attempt to be cheerful, her face was etched with sadness, and her eyes were dark and sunken. She gave Devon her hand, which felt cold.

"To the contrary, señora, I feel that I have helped bring grief upon you. I am sorry to see you have to suffer so."

"It is the will of God," she said. "He commands in all things."

"That is true. But your sadness still gives me pain." After a couple of seconds of pause, he went on. "I am also sorry to say that I come today to say good-bye."

The expression on her face softened. "Oh, are you going back to your own land?"

"With regrets, yes."

"And you are finished with your work here?"

"For now, yes."

"Well, it is sad that you are going, but if you should realize one or more paintings of what you have seen here, we would love to see them and perhaps to have one."

"Indeed. If I were to paint, I would come back to do it, and so you would be the first to see the work."

"Then you may not do a painting."

"It is possible. But even at that, I do not

have to have the motive of painting in order to return for a visit."

"Oh, that's the important thing." She gave him her hand again. "You will forgive me, señor, but I have many things to do inside. Thank you for coming, and please remember that you are always welcome at this house."

"Thank you very much, Doña Emilia."

As the sad lady went back into the house, Devon turned to Petra, who was standing close by in the shade of the *portal.* He saw she was not wearing earrings, a point of contrast that added to the austere mood of the day. He waited for her to speak.

"And so you are leaving before you finish your work?"

"Not really. As I told you last night, I feel that I have done as much as I am going to do on this trip."

"We have ruined your work for you."

"No, not at all. I believe my work has spoken to me and has told me, 'Enough, now.' "

"Oh? Do you think it is your destiny, then, not to paint a picture or pictures of the church?"

"Who knows? But not on this trip."

"Then you did not fulfill what you came for."

"Actually, I believe I did. I was looking for something, and I wasn't sure what. I had the illusion that I was going to find my vision, and I didn't. But I did learn that I was not going to find it all at once, all in one place."

"And there was another part, wasn't there?"

"Oh, yes. I thought that the complete vision would give me the ability to go back into my life with more power to act, but in reality I believe I have recovered that anyway."

"The ability."

"Yes. Although I did not find a full vision, I have experienced some things here that have made a difference in how I see life, and I imagine that if I try to find another place that offers peace and solitude, I will probably find something there worth seeing as well."

"In fragments."

"In parts, yes. And depending on how life looks to me after I've been gone from here for a while, I might come back this way, for one motive or another."

"You know that you are always welcome at Rancho Agua Prieta."

"Thank you. It is an honor."

As she gave him her hand again, her eyes

met his. They were dark, but softer than before.

"It is an honor for us to have your friendship," she said. "May God care for you on your trip."

"Thank you. And may God support you and your mother as you make your way through this difficult time."

"Thank you, señor *artista*."

He made a slight bow, then turned and went out into the bright day. He felt a tightness in his throat as he put on his hat and walked to the hitching rail. After untying the horses and turning them, he looked toward the *portal* and saw Petra in the doorway with her hand raised.

He waved back, then got his reins and lead rope in place and swung aboard. As the saddle horse lined out, he looked back at the packhorse and caught another wave from Petra. He moved his head to toss her a wave with his hat brim; then he rode across the yard, past the dark pool and shading cottonwood trees, through the stone gateway, and onto the plains. As the horse set out northward, he tipped his hat to the best of Rancho Agua Prieta, Dark Water Ranch.

317

ABOUT THE AUTHOR

John D. Nesbitt lives in the plains country of Wyoming, where he teaches English and Spanish at Eastern Wyoming College in Torrington. His Western stories have appeared in many magazines and anthologies. He has written many traditional Western novels, including *One-Eyed Cowboy Wild, Coyote Trail, Man from Wolf River,* and *For the Norden Boys;* more traditional Westerns are forthcoming. Two contemporary Western novels, *Keep the Wind in Your Face* and *A Good Man to Have in Camp,* keep company with *Antelope Sky* and *Seasons in the Fields,* two collections of contemporary Western short stories. Nesbitt has also brought out a collection of traditional Western short stories, *One Foot in the Stirrup,* and *Adventures of the Ramrod Rider,* a medley of parody, satire, poetry, and pristine romance. His fiction, nonfiction, book reviews, and poetry have been widely published. He has won many prizes and awards for his work, including a Wyoming Arts Council literary fellowship for his fiction writing, two awards from Wyoming Writers for encouragement of and service to other writers, and two fiction awards from the Wyoming State Historical Society.

The employees of Thorndike Press hope you have enjoyed this Large Print book. All our Thorndike, Wheeler, and Kennebec Large Print titles are designed for easy reading, and all our books are made to last. Other Thorndike Press Large Print books are available at your library, through selected bookstores, or directly from us.

For information about titles, please call:
(800) 223-1244

or visit our Web site at:
http://gale.cengage.com/thorndike

To share your comments, please write:
Publisher
Thorndike Press
295 Kennedy Memorial Drive
Waterville, ME 04901